Death By Bridle

A Josiah Reynolds Mystery

To Tammy
Thanks for [...]!
Abigail

Abigail Keam

Worker Bee Press

www.abigailkeam.com

Worker Bee Press
P.O. Box 485
Nicholasville, KY 40340

Acknowledgements

The author wishes to thank Al's Bar, which consented to be used as a drinking hole for my poetry-writing cop, Kelly, and Morris Book Shop, www.morrisbookshop.com, which consented to be a meeting place for Meriah Caldwell and Josiah in the series.

Special thanks to Daniel Considine, of Considine Farm Inc., for his special insight into the horse business and allowing access to horse breeding and racing facilities.
Also to Benita "Bunny" Lancaster for her help as well.
Special thanks must be given to Lucy Breathitt
for her oral history of Al Capone's sister.

Thanks to my beekeeping buddy, Clay Guthrie,
for letting me use him as a real person in a fictional work.

Thanks to my editor, Brian Throckmorton.

To the Lexington Farmers' Market,
which has given me a home for many years.
www.lexingtonfarmersmarket.com

Art Work by Cricket Press
www.cricket-press.com

Book Jacket by Peter Keam
With much gratitude.

By The Same Author

Death By A HoneyBee

Readers' Favorite Gold Medal Award 2010
Finalist of USA Book News Best Books of 2011

Death By Drowning

Readers' Favorite Gold Medal Award 2011
Finalist of USA Book News Best Books of 2011

Death By Bourbon
Coming Soon!

To Rebecca, Timothy, and Aaron

www.abigailkeam.com

Prologue

A door slammed.

Nine-year-old Lincoln Warfield Clark Todd was sleeping comfortably atop several bales of hay next to the stall of his mother's Thoroughbred stallion, Comanche, when the horse began pawing and snorting.

He thought little of it, as the black stallion was always restless and skittish. It wasn't until the horse began kicking his stall door that Linc sat up from his makeshift bed and rubbed his sleepy hazel eyes. "Whoa, boy. Nothing's gonna hurt ya while Linc's here," he murmured softly to the horse. "Go back to sleep."

It was then that he heard two loud voices coming from deep within the race-training complex. He looked at his cell phone. It was 2:30 in the morning. Linc crept over to soothe the horse by rubbing his velvety muzzle.

"Quiet, Comanche," Linc commanded the big Thoroughbred.

Both horse and boy strained to listen. Comanche's ears lay flat against his gleaming black coat. Linc held onto the horse's bridle as he wondered where the night watchman was. Probably watching TV in the owner's office.

A chair scraped across concrete. The voices became louder and more argumentative. A man called the other a "son-of-a-bitch" and said "you'll ruin me."

The young boy, heavy with excitement, crept forward among the hanging tack, leaning rakes, stacked bales of hay, and black plastic buckets stuffed with brushes, combs, and hoof picks. Peeking around the corner he chewed on his lower lip, a habit his mother was trying to get him to quit.

At the far end of the stable corridor, two men stood facing each other like gunfighters. He couldn't see them very well as only one yellow light glowed feebly from the ceiling. Horses poked their shaggy heads out of their stalls, their walnut eyeballs wide and glassy with foreboding.

A washed-out-looking man drew his fists up, crying, "I'll kill you if you tell. I'll kill you. I swear I will." A single light, dangling from a worn-out cord, swung slightly from a light breeze, creating eerie dancing shadows on the man's gray flesh. He fumbled towards the other man, who raised his arms in defense.

A spike of fear ran up Linc's back. He rose from his crouching position, gasping.

Both men swiveled, staring at him with dumbfounded irritation. One of the men thudded towards Linc. The young boy ran in the opposite direction, but fell over a feed bucket, cracking his head on the concrete floor. His world went black.

It stayed black for a very long time.

1

Shaneika called at seven that morning, relating that Linc was in the hospital and asking me to come right away.

"I'll be there," I mumbled, wiping the sleep from my eyes. Pushing away Baby, my fawn English mastiff, I untangled myself from the bed sheets but Shaneika hung up before I could ask any questions.

I called my best friend Matt at his law office, informing him of the morning's call. Both he and Shaneika were my lawyers, often working together. Matt asked that I keep him apprised of the situation. He replied that he had to go after I heard someone calling his name.

A woman. Hmmmm. I recognized that friendly sexy tone of voice and knew what it meant, but couldn't bother to think of that now.

Looking for Jake, I found him swimming laps in the heated infinity pool. Jake had been my bodyguard/physician's assistant since my fall from a cliff when a rogue cop tried to kill me. That's a long story, one that I want to forget, but the cop is still on the loose.

My daughter assigned Jake to me. He really works for her.

Somewhere along the line, I crossed the no-no boundary and fell in love with Jake. But I have nothing to offer. I'm much older. My body is put together with glue and wire. I don't think it could survive a younger man's attention. What little money I have is tied up in paying medical bills and keeping my farm afloat. So when his contract is up this October, I'm going to send Jake away.

By the way, my name is Josiah Reynolds. My grandmother named me after a Hebrew king known for his righteousness.

I'm known for other things, not all of them nice.

Previously an art history professor, I now keep honeybees and sell honey at the Farmers' Market in Lexington, Kentucky. It's enough to get by on if I live on the cheap. I'll never get rich on honeybees. It's more a work of love.

I clutched my robe at the throat while leaning over the steaming water to get Jake's attention. He rose up like Nix, the Norse god of lakes – water streaming from his long, blue-black hair and down his ruddy, muscular body. "What's up," he asked, wiping hair from his eyes. He looked at me from under thick, dark eyelashes.

The pool wasn't the only thing steaming.

"Shaneika called. Said her boy was in the hospital. Wants me to come. Can you drive?"

"Sure thing. Why's he in the hospital?"

"Don't know. Just told me he was and asked me to hurry."

"Okay, but you do your exercises first, have breakfast, take your medication and then we'll go."

I shook my head. "That will take too long. She wants me to come now."

Jake scowled. "I don't care what she wants. You're still on a medical schedule. You don't know how strenuous a day this will be. You'll need your therapy and medication to make sure you can endure today without a lot of pain."

The magic word – pain.

I was terrified of pain and would do most anything to avoid it. We never fight except about my pain medication. I want more – lots more of the pain medication – not the pain.

He was right and I knew it. I dropped my robe and, in my jammies, got into the warm water. We did a half hour of stretching before Jake sent me to the showers while he made breakfast and got dressed himself. Within minutes, we were racing towards the hospital.

2

Linc's skin was ashen as he lay in the hospital bed with tubes placed in various orifices. It didn't look good.

"What happened?" I asked, touching Linc's forehead. He felt cool.

Shaneika stood at the foot of the bed with her arms folded tightly. "Nobody knows. Nobody will tell me anything. That's why I called. I need help. I got a call from the guard at the Royal Blue Stables letting me know that Linc was hurt, but not how. Police have been milling around this floor since we got here. I don't think Linc's injuries are accidental, but nobody will talk to me. Something is going on. Please help me, Josiah. I can't leave here, but you can ask around," she pleaded in her English clip. She had spent many years in Bermuda.

Jake interjected, "Mrs. Reynolds is in no position to play sleuth. She is still healing from her . . ."

"Don't give me that," snapped Shaneika. She pointed a finger at me. "I've done nothing but favors for you.

Now I want some payback." Her hazel eyes burned madly.

When I didn't respond, Shaneika began to cry. "I'm so sorry, but I need some answers and need them quick. What is going on? How'd this happen to my baby?"

I sighed. It hadn't been that long since Irene Meckler had asked me to nose around her nephew's death. I was still recovering from my fall and was exhausted, frankly. Still I said, "I will see what I can do, but no promises."

"But," interrupted Jake, looking frantically at us both.

I held up my hand to silence him. Turning to Shaneika, I said, "Keep me apprised if you hear anything and I will do the same." I limped out of the hospital room on my black ebony cane with the silver wolf's head.

Jake followed hotly on my heels. "Now listen, Boss Lady, you're in no shape to go traipsing around the countryside. Remember the agony you were in poking around the Dunne case."

I nodded. He was right. But I couldn't sit comfortably at home when people who had taken risks for me now asked for help. I was obligated to Shaneika. And obligated people with a sense of honor rise to the occasion.

Social critic Thomas Sowell said, "One of the common failings among honorable people is a failure to appreciate how thoroughly dishonorable some other people can be, and how dangerous it is to trust them."

This advice was not lost on me as I had discovered the depths of people's depravity, but only recently.

As Matt's boyfriend, Franklin, told me, "You have poor risk assessment."

So do most people.

3

Jake drove over to the Royal Blue Stables, which was crawling with cops. We couldn't even get through the gate. So I had Jake take me to Al's Bar, a gritty little nook on the corner of Limestone and Sixth where writers and the disenfranchised hung out. It was now closed to the public, but I knew the back door would be open. I walked into the dimly lit joint where a few workers were restocking and cleaning.

One of them looked up, brandishing a soapy bar rag. "Hey man, we're closed."

"It's cool. I just want to talk to Kelly," I replied. The bartender grunted and went about her work. Officer Kelly looked up at the mention of his name and studied me as I walked towards him. His table was scattered with crumpled-up papers where he had been laboring over a new poem. He brushed them onto the floor.

"Stumped?" I asked, sitting down on a decrepit bench.

He rubbed a freckled hand through his auburn hair. "I think I have writer's block. I just can't get this latest poem right. Maybe I'm tired." He gathered his other papers together and placed them in a notebook. "You didn't come down here to discuss poetry. Whaddya need?" He motioned to the bartender. "Get this lady a Coke and some chips. Got any soup ready?"

I smiled. Kelly always wanted to feed me. It was precious.

"How's Baby?" asked Kelly.

I thanked the girl who placed a Coke and a cup of chili before me. I looked around for some crackers. "He's fine. Growing like a weed. He's put on another twenty-five pounds," I replied about my mastiff, which Kelly had saved after O'nan had tried to kill Baby . . . and me – but that's another story. "I'm still taking him to obedience school, but he's dumb as a rock. He won't even sit when commanded."

"Dumb as a fox," Kelly retorted. "Baby's just willful and lazy. He acts stupid so there won't be any expectations of him, but he's smart. Make no mistake about that."

I took a sip of my drink. "When did you become a dog whisperer?" I put some crackers in my steaming chili and inhaled its spicy aroma.

Kelly nodded to Jake, who was sitting at the bar nursing a beer. Jake nodded back, but kept watching both front and back doors. The bartender flirted with Jake until he gave her a rigid stare. She scurried away, leaving him alone.

"I'm good at reading things. You know that," answered Kelly. "Like I can read that you are nervous and need something – something that you think I can provide. And Sitting Bull over there is pissed off. I would guess at you. I would also venture to say you two have got something going on because he's got that boyfriend kind of pissed-off look."

Kelly gave me a wicked grin. "Well, well. You're blushing and I was just fishing."

"His name is Jacob Dosh and he's my bodyguard."

Kelly shrugged. "If you say so."

"My lawyer, Shaneika Mary Todd, called me this morning to tell me that her son is in a coma after being found unconscious at the Royal Blue Stables. I went over there and the place is crawling with cops. No one will tell her anything – so she asked me to find out. Linc's a good boy and his mother has been a huge help to me for the past year."

"I know who Shaneika Todd is. I have had several run-ins with her in court. She's not very well liked by the police department. She keeps getting scumbags off."

"She's a criminal lawyer and does her job well."

"That she does," sighed Kelly, "and it's probably why no one is talking to her. They want to make her sweat a little bit."

"You don't play games like that where children are concerned."

"I agree. So that's why I am going to tell you what happened . . . but you didn't hear it here."

I crossed my heart. "Scout's honor."

Kelly leaned forward. "Lincoln may have witnessed a murder. That's why we're hanging around his room. Protection . . . see."

"Who was murdered?"

"Arthur Aaron Greene III. He was found hanging from one of the rafters, but he had been strangled with a horse's bridle which was still wrapped around his neck."

I reared back in my bench seat, stunned for a moment.

Arthur Aaron Greene III was huge in the Thoroughbred racing industry, having bred several champions including a Kentucky Derby winner. I knew him through Lady Elsmere, my neighbor, who shared the same horse racing enthusiasm. He was a great friend of hers.

Kelly continued. "That's all I know at the moment. I'm not on the case."

"Who's the primary?"

"Your good friend, Goetz."

I threw down my napkin. "Whew, this chili is good, but too hot. You want it?"

"Yeah, give it here."

I scooted the bowl over and fished for some money in my pocket.

"Don't insult me," said Kelly waving me away. "After all the meals I ate at your place when Asa and I were dating. Hell, I practically lived at your house then."

I smiled. "Those were wonderful days, weren't they?"

Kelly's green eyes grew soft. "Yeah, Josiah, those were wonderful days. I know it's a cliché, but life was golden. We just didn't know it."

His voice grew raspy as he remembered. "Asa and I would work on the farm during the morning and ride horses or go boating all afternoon. We'd come in and you'd have this big dinner waiting for us – always out on the patio. Mr. Reynolds would come home and change into some kind of caftan and flip-flops. He was always telling jokes.

"I thought you were so sophisticated. The two of you would have cocktails before dinner and play old jazz records on a big old-fashioned console. We'd eat and watch the sun go down together."

I joined in. "Then you, Asa, and I would go for a late night swim. We'd sit in the pool and talk, listening to the owls and watching the stars twirl 'round in the sky."

"That's when you smoked," laughed Kelly. "You would sit on the pool steps smoking one cigarette right after another, telling us stories about history and art."

I joined in his laugher. "When Brannon and I started out it was all hearts and diamonds, then it turned to clubs and spades."

Kelly gave me a quick smile. "You know I write because of you."

I cocked my head. "Really?"

"I remember you saying that each individual had a responsibility to do something beautiful in his or her life, even if it was painting a horse fence. The quest for beauty kept us from becoming enamored of evil."

"Oh dear, I don't think I could have said anything that profound."

"You did. I'll swear to it," whispered Kelly touching my fingers with his. We smiled at each other remembering the wonderful times we had shared.

21

As my eyes began to tear, a clean handkerchief was thrust in front of me. I twisted in my booth seat to see Jake, frowning and towering over me.

"She cries at the drop of a hat now," said Jake. "A squirrel crosses the road in front of the car and she begins to cry."

"Damn it, we were having a moment," I snapped. "And I cry because I'm happy the squirrel made it to the other side. Life is fragile."

"I'm Jake Dosh," said Jake, extending a thick hand that was scarred and nicked. Though he didn't look it because he was so wiry, Jake was incredibly strong. Once he had leaned over a boat's side, lifting me from the ocean with one hand. Holding me suspended in air, he dropped me back into the water when a shark lost interest. And that was when I was quite chunky. Oh hell, let's call it what it was – I was fat, very fat.

After my husband, Brannon had left me for a younger woman, I had gone on a three-year eating binge. Only after the "accident" did I lose weight, and not because I wanted to.

Kelly shook Jake's hand and invited him to sit. His emerald green eyes gave Jake the once-over, taking in his clothes, age, physique, and obviously the weapon under his shirt. Jake gave Kelly the same appraisal. He gave Kelly a look that said he was the new gun in town.

"Naw, man. We gotta go," barked Jake, helping me to my feet. He handed me my cane. "Say goodbye, Josiah."

Kelly grabbed my hand and whispered so that Jake couldn't hear. "Be careful, Miss Josiah. Arthur was found with stones in his pockets and a bucket of water underneath him." He looked around to see if anyone was listening. "Look for the widow's son."

With that, he stood. "Hey, Dosh!"

Jake turned around. "Yeah, man?"

"Keep her safe, will ya."

Jake's golden brown eyes flickered for a brief second and then narrowed. "Do my best, hoss."

4

We stopped the car in front of Lady Elsmere's door, which was immediately opened by Charles, her African-American butler. He ushered us in but not before I brushed against a black wreath on the door. As Charles escorted us to the back terrace, I noticed black chiffon had been draped over all the mirrors.

Jake hung back. "What's with the coverings over the mirrors?"

"So the soul of the departed doesn't get trapped behind the mirrors. Mirrors are considered portals. It was originally a Roman custom. Reflective water also had to be covered in the ancient world after death as well as coins put on the eyelids for payment to the ferryman, Charon. Southern people still cover mirrors as well as Jews who do it out of respect for the dead. Some Europeans put coins on the eyes to this day," I replied.

"Okey dokey," replied Jake rubbing his chin. He was

not impressed.

Charles noticed my noticing. "She got word this morning about Mr. Greene's death. It's been quite a shock for her. So please, go softly."

"What's with the mourning display? She's not his widow," I admonished curtly. "Only the house of the deceased is supposed to cover the mirrors."

I sometimes despised Lady Elsmere's sense of drama. It set my teeth on edge.

Ever loyal, Charles said nothing, but just shook his head as he opened the glass double doors to the brick terrace and announced me.

June, sucking on a whisky soda, motioned me to sit beside her with a frail but diamond-laden hand. It looked like a claw dripping with glitter. She was wearing a bright yellow pantsuit with a black mourning band encircling the upper left arm. Her eyes looked red from crying and she had forgotten to pencil in her eyebrows. She looked drunk, sick, and eyebrowless. "Bring Josiah something," begged Lady Elsmere to Charles. "What do you want, dear?"

I shook my head.

"Bring her a Bloody Mary," cackled June.

"No thank you, Charles. I won't be here that long."

"Bring some hot tea then with some of her honey."

Charles gave a quick little nod and was gone like a puff of smoke.

Opening an antique gold case, June took a ciggy out. She tapped it on the patio table and looked out upon her vast back pastures that held grazing Thoroughbreds.

"Do you know how old I am?" asked June as I bent to light her cigarette with a gem-studded lighter from the table.

Were those real rubies and diamonds?

"Not really," I lied.

"I'm old enough to remember hemp being the major crop grown. Then that was outlawed and tobacco was king. Now that is gone too. Nothing left in the Bluegrass but horse breeders grabbing a fast buck and heirloom tomato farmers."

She spat out a fleck of tobacco. "This town used to be a place of grace and culture. Now it's a rat hole with a mall on every corner. Half the antebellum houses I used to visit have been torn down for subdivisions. Every time a field is paved over, a bit of our collective soul is chipped away until nothing will be left but rot. I hate the new Lexington. Hate it."

"You're being a little hard, aren't you?" I replied. My feelings were hurt since Brannon, my late husband, and I had built one of those subdivisions.

June ignored me as usual. "I heard it on the news. I was just finishing breakfast when they announced that Arthur had been brutally murdered. Murdered!" She took a deep draw and then exhaled a stream of smoke. "I never thought I'd outlive him. Never."

"The reason I am here, June, is that you were fond of Arthur and knew him for many years, but I am kind of surprised by how hard you're taking this. I don't mean to pry but you are acting like . . . I don't know, like a . . ."

"Like a wife. Like a lover." She turned, staring at me.

There was silence between us.

"Is there something I'm missing here?"

She gave me a knowing look.

"Uhmm, how connected were you and Arthur?"

"Arthur was the great love of my life."

I sat for a moment, taking in what June had just said. There was no use quitting now. The hat was out of the box. "Like a platonic admirer or are you talking about a lover as in sex?"

June puffed on her cigarette and said nothing.

"Jumping Jehosaphat!" I sat back in my chair, surprised. No one really thinks of old ladies having grand passions.

She arched the place where an eyebrow should have been. "That shocks you."

"I don't know what to say. I really am speechless. I mean, he was so much younger than you."

"Twenty-eight years to be exact. We met at the Rolex Event. He was forty-two and I was seventy. We were lovers for many years until I became too frail and then we became even better friends."

"Did his wife know?"

June spat out, "I don't know if she knows and don't give a big rat's fanny. I never cared. Arthur was my last chance for happiness and I took it."

She watched the trail of cigarette smoke dissipate. "I loved all my husbands, you know, but in different ways. My first husband was my high school sweetheart. Then Lord Elsmere . . . we were fond of each other, but he lived his life and I was left to live mine. He loved the ladies, but didn't like to love the ladies."

"He was what Thomas Jefferson referred to as a 'Miss Nancy'?"

"Yes, but he was very good to me. Made sure that I would be taken care of after his death." She paused as though remembering. "He had such a dry wit about him . . . and such a gentleman. Rather courtly manners. In the thirty-five years since his death, I've met only one man who is only a crude facsimile to my Bertie, and that is your Matt."

Charles came out with a tray and poured some hot tea into a cup for me. June waved him away impatiently.

I sipped on my tea, waiting for June to continue.

She continued to puff away.

"Then he dies and you come back home to Kentucky," I said, prodding her to the good part about the infidelity and sex.

"Years later I met Arthur at the Rolex Event and we just hit it off."

"Okay, you met Arthur at the Rolex Event in Lexington."

June looked at me with irritation written all over her pale, wrinkled face. "I just said that."

"Hey, it was less than a year ago that I got my skull cracked open, so if it takes me a little longer than most to get the facts straight, do forgive me, your majesty." I instantly regretted my words.

"Well, at least my loves died on me. I didn't throw love away like . . ."

28

"Like I did? Is that what you were going to say?"

June squared her shoulders and looked at me with spite. "You did that with Brannon. If you had asked him to come home, he would have, but you were too proud. You threw away a good marriage just because he wanted to play patty cake with some young thing for a while. Don't all men at some point?"

I stood, furious. "I guess not with you. Seemed like every time you needed a man, one popped up from nowhere. How convenient is that? How many seventy-year-old broads get another go-around with a man half her age and a married man at that? You never paid any consequences."

"You mean, paid for my sins? What rubbish that is."

"You make me so mad, June."

Lady Elsmere shrugged, "I thought you came to comfort me. All you want to do is to judge, and it's Lady Elsmere to you!" she cried, pointing a dragon claw at me.

"I came to ask some questions to help a friend. I didn't know that you were doing the nasty with the dead guy. Then you start busting my chops about Brannon. What the hell do you know about it, anyway? You think you're the only one who's ever shed a tear? I'm getting out of here."

June shushed me. "Go on then. I want to be alone with my memories anyway." She turned her back.

"That went well," I murmured.

Charles must have been watching as he opened the terrace door and beckoned. Once I was inside he confided, "She's been like this all morning. Drinkin' like

29

a fish. Cussing everybody out. Just hateful. Now she wants to go parading to that man's funeral with his family there. I'm afraid she'll say something to Mr. Arthur's wife and there will be a scandal. It's not fittin'. Not fittin'."

I placed my hand over my heart trying to calm its ragged thumping. "What a beating I just took. Let me think for a moment. Why don't you call her doctor and have him prescribe some sedatives to calm her nerves. If she still insists on going to the funeral, I'll offer to go with her."

"That's a good idea, Miss Josiah. I'll do just that. I've got my grandchildren stationed around the house to keep an eye on her. She won't be able to go to the bathroom without me knowing about it."

"Lady Elsmere's got a good friend in you, Charles."

"She's your good friend too, Miss Josiah. She doesn't know what she's saying. She's half out her mind with grief. You need to let this roll off your back."

"I know it, but she just knows how to push my buttons." I grabbed his arm.

"Charles, is it true what she told me about Arthur?"

Charles nodded.

"How could I have missed that? I was with them both many times and I never suspected their true relationship. I feel so dumb."

"They both wanted it kept very quiet."

"They did a good job. I was never even suspicious."

Charles did not reply.

"I'll take my leave then. Keep me informed, will you, Charles?" I told him about Lincoln and why I had come.

Charles assured me he would let me know of anything pertinent to Lincoln. His nut-brown face was full of concern as I left.

Jake was waiting for me in the grand staircase hallway. Seeing my strained face, he put his arm around my waist and helped me to the car. It felt good to lean into his hard body. "Here we go again . . . you doing too much."

"I know. I know."

"You hungry?"

"Nope."

"How's the pain doing?"

"Manageable at the moment. I can live with it."

"Well, that's a first. You go straight to bed. I'll call the hospital and talk to Shaneika. I heard everything Kelly told you. Maybe when you wake up, Linc will be up and about."

I reclined the car seat and was asleep before he drove out of the driveway.

5

When awakened from my nap, I heard Matt and Jake talking in the great room. I washed my face and combed my hair after changing from my wrinkled day clothes into a green silk caftan, which set off my eyes. I had to keep pushing the kittens, which were now sizable, away from my things as they thought this was a great opportunity to either crawl up my back or knock lipstick tubes off the vanity.

These were the progeny of a barn cat who had taken up residence in my clothes closet along with her boyfriend. She used my favorite cashmere sweater as a bed. I didn't have the heart to throw her and the family out until now.

"First opportunity, boys, and you're going to the barn," I threatened, picking up a black and white kitten trying to chew my hairbrush. I kissed his nose.

Baby padded in, gave me a brief nod and went into the bathroom so he could drink out of the toilet. He looked up in annoyance as I scolded him. "You have fresh bowls of water in the kitchen and outside. Yet you insist on drinking out of my toilet. It's disgusting."

Water dripped from his massive face folds only to be followed by strings of drool. I tried to wipe his face off with a towel but he fought, so I gave up. I didn't want to risk falling. Baby, knowing that he had won the battle, burped and thudded out of the bathroom, no doubt on the prowl for something to eat. The kittens skedaddled after him in delight. Whatever he got to eat, Baby shared with them calmly, if not happily.

Finally at peace in my own bedroom suite, I put on some makeup. I looked in the mirror satisfied. I was ready to see Matt, who was the most gorgeous human being I had ever beheld. He strongly resembled Victor Mature, the matinee idol of the forties and fifties. Dark thick wavy hair, piercing blue eyes that accentuated a Roman patrician nose. Pronounced lips that gave way to a strong chin and jawbone. Wide shoulders tapered to a narrow waist and then jutted out to perfectly sculpted thighs and calves. Yes, indeedy, Matt had won the genetic jackpot.

I ventured into the great room without Jake and Matt knowing, for they were deep in conversation. I couldn't help but compare them. Jake looked like a scrappy mutt next to Matt's cultured looks but that still had its attractions. Jake was not as tall but his body looked powerful with its sinewy muscles. His hair was also black but longer and thicker with a blue tint to it. While Matt's features were refined, Jake's were blunt and the skin seemed stretched tightly across his skull, but somehow the features worked together to make Jake look rough and sexy while Matt looked beautiful, yet cold and unapproachable.

Both men were hard workers. Both men were confident in their abilities, but that's where it ended. Matt had had a classical education and spoke Latin with ease. We both loved art, vintage movies, and fine clothes. We paid homage to beauty.

Jake could have cared less about art. His training had been in the Marines and medicine. He was practical and observant, making those hard decisions about life from which Matt and I shied away.   Jake loved nature and understood how to keep balance with it, but as much as he loved life he could take it easily. For him death was a part of life.

Matt was always brooding about the big questions of life. Jake already understood them.

I cleared my throat, causing them to look up.

Matt smiled when he saw me. He must have been pleased, as he liked me to dress up a little bit. It had given him great pleasure when he and Franklin, his boyfriend, had raided my closet while I was in Key West and burned all my stained, torn, and faded shirts and pants. Franklin even raided my underwear drawer and replaced my granny underwear and bras with cute little lacy things that were totally impractical to wear in my condition . . . or at my age.

34

I walked over to a chair and slowly sat.

"Where's your cane, Josiah?" asked Matt.

"I'm only using it when I go out. I feel confident walking in the house."

Matt looked pleased. "Well, that's another improvement, isn't it, Jake?"

"I think she's doing better and better each day. Pain seems to be under control," he said.

"For now," I interjected.

"For now," Jake repeated. "She's sleeping better and we've cut down on a lot of medication. She's not a pill jockey anymore. Going in the right direction." He smiled at me.

I knew he was pleased at his part in my recovery as well. Indeed, my improved health was largely due to him.

"What were you guys discussing?" I asked.

Matt scratched his arm. "I went to the hospital after work. The good thing is that Linc is awake, but he refuses to say anything . . . even to his mother. And Shaneika's having a time keeping the cops out of the room."

"I would have to agree with her on that. Linc needs time to recover."

"But the cops want to talk with him while his thoughts and impressions are fresh," said Jake. "They don't want him to have time to lock in on any false memories."

"Are they still guarding his room?"

Matt nodded. "I talked to one of the cops on duty. They are taking this case very seriously and really think Linc might be in some kind of danger. It would remove significant threat if Linc would give an official statement. Otherwise they think the killer might make a move on him."

"Hell's bells," I whispered. I struggled to stand up. Jake held Matt back from helping me.

"Struggling is part of the process," cautioned Jake.

Personally, I would have liked to have had help.

"I am going to make some dishes, and Jake – you're going to help me."

Matt raised an eyebrow. "This is the first time you've cooked since the accident." We always refer to O'nan pulling me off the cliff and falling forty feet as the "accident."

"I think if Jake helps me, I can do it. You go home and relax for a while. Then you and Franklin come back around 7:30 for dinner. If I do well, we'll eat here. If not, we'll go out."

Rubbing his hands together with glee, Matt asked, "What are you going to cook?"

"None of your beeswax. It will be simple. Nothing grand. Now scoot," I said. "I'll see you later."

Jake procured a swivel barstool and placed it by the counter where I had put out juicy tomatoes, several different kinds of cheeses, bread, sliced turkey. "Jake, I need you to fry some bacon but not too crispy."

"What are you making?"

"Ever eaten a Hot Brown?"

"Nope, never heard of such a thing."

"A Hot Brown is a thing of beauty, of symmetry. Fred Schmidt, who worked for Louisville's Brown Hotel in 1926, created it. It was to be a signature late evening dish catering to those who weaved into the hotel after a night of dancing and other carousing. Every Kentuckian eats a Hot Brown now and then. Keeps the bad cholesterol up."

"I can see that," replied Jake, looking dubiously at the cheese and bacon. "How many fat grams does this thing have?"

"Hush. A Hot Brown is a work of art. Besides, it's Linc's favorite meal."

"Ahh, I see. A little bribery may be in the offing."

"If the Hot Browns come out well, I think I should pay Linc a visit tomorrow."

"Around lunch time?"

"Definitely."

I told Jake where to find the Bybee plates I always used to make Hot Browns. After he washed them and placed them by me, we both worked quietly in the kitchen. We seemed to anticipate each other's moves, so it was easy and dinner was in the oven in twenty minutes. In another ten minutes, we had my prized Nakashima table set with several bottles of chilled white wine.

Satisfied with our accomplishment, we eyed the table with pleasure and then smiled at each other. We held each other's eyes longer than necessary. I felt the blood rush to my face.

"If you could start cooking here and there, that would take a lot of pressure off me," said Jake, breaking the tension.

I nodded. "They would have to be very simple . . .
and I would need help getting to certain dishes and pans."

"Why don't you make a list and I'll get the ingredients.
We'll spend a day making dishes that we can freeze for
later use. It will save us time cooking every day."

Happy that I might be able to contribute even on a
small scale gave me something to look forward to. I
planned to make a complete list the next day.

An hour or so later, Matt and Franklin straggled in,
looking apprehensive until I pulled the spotted blue and
white dishes out of the oven. Matt placed them on the
table.

"Yummy," said Franklin, who jumped in his seat while
pulling his napkin out of the wine glass. "I'll take a little
vino too, please."

Matt poured lemon water into my glass. I made a face
but didn't complain. I was still on medication that would
not allow me to drink alcohol. Jake placed my cane on
the back of my chair and sat beside me. The Hot Browns
gave off a wonderful aroma and were steaming from the
still bubbling cheeses.

Franklin stood up, holding his wine glass. "I would
like to make a toast to our lovely hostess who now feels
well enough to cook wonderful dishes for the men in her
life."

Matt and Jake took spoons to their wine glasses.
"Hear, hear," they echoed.

"And who also promised me several months ago, that
when the time was right, she would invite me and Lady

Elsmere to a dinner party at the Butterfly. Remember that?" asked Franklin, pursing his lips.

"Sit down, Franklin," admonished Matt.

"Well, she did."

"I would like to say that this is Josiah's first cooked meal since the accident. We wish her a full recovery and much happiness in the years to come."

Jake winked at me. "Like the sound of that."

Everyone took a sip including myself. I looked at their shining faces and knew that I was beaming.

It came as a shock then, that in less than fifteen hours, my world would crumble and I would lose the man I loved.

6

I entered the heated pool, which was steaming in the morning's brisk air. Jake had already done his laps and stood holding water weights. The sun was skirting the top of the trees as songbirds flitted to the various bird feeders stationed near the patio. I noticed a red cardinal, the state bird, sharing a meal along with an American goldfinch plus a nuthatch and black-capped chickadee. A flicker bounced from one walnut tree to another.

Jake handed me weights, instructing me to do some jumping jacks in the shallow end. I obeyed. Jake jumped out to get some more exercise equipment.

The air was nippy so I moved into the deeper water so my shoulders would be covered. My feet slipped and I went under. I don't know what happened. I guess I panicked. I just kept sliding into deeper water as I tried to get my bearings.

I felt a hand grab my hair and pull me up. My arms flailed for the poolside until my hands made contact with something solid.

"Damn," sputtered Jake as I spat out water. "I can't turn my back for a moment."

I pushed the hair out of my eyes. "I slipped."

"You're always going to slip or fall with that bum leg of yours. You gotta stay calm and think about what to do when falling. You've got to stop this panicking every time you go down or you will never be independent. Never."

Seeing the fear on my face, he relented and said, "Let me check you out." He put his arms around me and pulled me to the shallow end. Clinging with my arms around his neck, I pressed against him. Jake looked down.

I felt the sun beating down on my face as I met his gaze.

Suddenly he was kissing me. I held him tighter, greedily meeting his kiss. Time felt suspended as I drank in the touch of his lips, his muscular arms around me, the feel of his bare torso against mine.

A kiss can be a powerful thing. It can open up worlds. It can heal. I felt as though I was drowning again but this time I didn't care. I would surrender to wherever it took me.

"MOTHER!"

Both Jake and I jerked our heads up.

There stood Asa, my daughter, standing by the pool's edge looking . . . I don't know . . . surprised?

Feeling like I had been caught necking by my mother, I giggled. Jake jumped out of the pool and pulled me with him. He wrapped a towel around me, nodded to Asa, and then fled to his bedroom.

I gave my daughter a big hug. "What are you doing here?"

"I've got some good news for you and wanted to tell you in person." She beckoned to the patio table and chairs. "Are you warm enough?"

"Sure. You've met someone and getting married?" I asked hopefully.

Asa resisted rolling her eyes. "Nooooo. O'nan's been caught and is now behind bars without bail for the moment, but I doubt any judge would give him bail. He's too much of a flight risk."

I clasped Asa's hands. "How, when . . . oh this is good news."

"We traced him to France and had Interpol pick him up. For once the French are going to cooperate and extradite him. He'll be in Lexington's hands soon. He'll never hurt you again, Mom. Never."

"He'll go to jail and stay there?"

"Unless something screwy happens, he'll be behind bars for a long time."

"Praise God," I responded and smiled warmly at my dark-haired, dark-eyed daughter. She had her father's fine features.

"Let's get you into some dry clothes. You look like you're shivering to me."

"I am trembling from all the excitement this morning."

She lifted an eyebrow but said nothing.

"Oh, have I got something to tell you about June too."

Asa laughed. "I hope it's juicy, but tell me after you're dressed."

"I was going to take a Hot Brown to Linc at the hospital before lunch. You want to go with me?"

"Yes, Shaneika called and told me what happened. I wish you wouldn't get involved. Let me handle it."

I shook my head. "I can't refuse after all that she has done for me."

Asa hesitated for a moment but nodded in agreement. "See your point." Changing the subject, she continued, "I need to talk some stuff over with Jake. Why don't you have my driver take you and then I'll meet you for lunch and bring you back home?"

"Sounds okay. I'm sure Jake would like the time off. Have the car brought around in an hour. I'll be ready then."

"Sure. I'll put my bag in my room and then I'll join you in the kitchen before you leave for the hospital."

Asa gave me a quick hug and petted Baby, who kept nuzzling her hand. He thumped after her while I went to take a quick shower and change, but not before I put a Hot Brown in the oven.

Within an hour and half, I was in Lincoln Warfield Clark Todd's room bribing him with the Hot Brown and some chocolate milk. A wide smile spread across his light brown face. I told him quite frankly that the food was a bribe and he would not get a bite unless he spilled all that he knew.

Linc sang like a bird.

The story boiled down to two white men arguing to the point of physical blows until they noticed him. He told me that he got scared and while trying to get away fell over a feed bucket. That's all that he remembered. "Am I in trouble, Mrs. Reynolds? I didn't mean to knock over that feed bucket. I'll pay for the oats."

I gave Linc a quick hug. "Sweetie, you're not in trouble. You did nothing wrong."

"Then why is everyone acting so creepy around me . . . and those policemen keep hanging around my door?"

I realized that no one had told Linc. "One of the men got hurt. The police just want to make sure that you don't get hurt as well." I playfully pinched his cheek.

Linc laughed and pushed my hand away.

"Linc, do you think you could recognize those men if you saw pictures of them?"

Linc looked thoughtful after he sipped his chocolate milk. "I think so." He looked eagerly at me. "I could try." He handed me his empty milk carton. "Is that man okay?"

"No, Linc, that man got hurt real bad. So anything you can remember will be helpful."

His gentle hazel eyes widened.

"But remember, it's not your fault. If you can't remember anything else, that's okay too. The most important thing is that you get better soon."

"I'm getting out as soon as the doctor checks on me today."

"That's great," I replied, putting the empty dish into my basket.

"Is that man going to get better?" questioned Linc again, looking at me with concern.

At first I paused, not knowing the right thing to say. Then I said, "Don't you worry about it. You just concentrate on you." I gave him my best smile.

"Okay, Mrs. Reynolds."

"See you later, Linc."

Lincoln cheerfully waved goodbye.

As soon as I shut the door, Shaneika and Detective Goetz were on me like ticks on an old beagle howling in the brush for rabbits. "Let's stand over here where Linc can't see or hear us," I cautioned, pointing to an empty waiting room.

"Well," demanded Goetz impatiently.

I gave them both a succinct report of exactly what Linc had told me. I also told them that I didn't tell Linc that a man was dead. We weren't even sure at this point if one of the men he had seen was Arthur Greene.

Goetz wrote furiously in his little notebook before looking at me. "Do you think he knows anything else?"

I shrugged. "Maybe a therapist could get more out of him, but he was pretty relaxed. I think he told me everything he remembered."

"What about recognizing the men? When can I bring him some pictures?"

Shaneika seethed. "He's done. Got that."

Goetz turned toward her, his big belly almost rubbing up against her. "He is the witness to a murder where a man was hung from a barn rafter. Keeping this information to himself will only place him in danger."

Shaneika stuck a finger in Goetz's face. "See here, you big . . ."

"Whoa. Let's all simmer down," I advised, stepping between them. "Shaneika, what do you plan to do when Linc is released today?"

Not taking her eyes from Goetz's face, she answered, "I was going to take him to his grandmother's in Versailles."

"She got any protection there?" asked Goetz.

Shaneika responded, "Well, no, but everybody knows everyone else on that street. If some stranger comes around, people will know it."

"What were you going to do with Comanche?" I asked.

"I was going to bring him back to the Butterfly since O'nan got picked up," she answered looking sheepishly.

"That's a good idea," interrupted my daughter who rounded the corner. "I've got a plan that will suit everyone. The Butterfly is protected 24/7 and there's lots of room. Why don't you bring Lincoln to the house until this blows over?"

If Shaneika was surprised to see Asa, she didn't act it. "Let me think on it," she answered.

"You and your mother can stay as well. Security is already built in and the refrigerator is stocked full of food."

"That might not be a bad idea," I interrupted while mentally counting how many extra beds I had. "I have lots of albums with pictures of Arthur Greene in them. I can go through them with Linc and see if he recognizes him." And I turned to Goetz, "And you can place a police car by the driveway entrance."

Goetz rubbed his chin. "This might work."

"Shaneika, you can go to work knowing that there are several layers of protection around Lincoln," coaxed Asa.

I reassured Shaneika. "I've got plenty of room, really I do. It will be very little bother."

"What do you think?" asked Shaneika of Goetz.

"I think Josiah's home is a fortress. All the security mistakes that were made with O'nan have been corrected. No one can get in unless somebody makes a stupid error in judgment. I'd take her up on the offer."

"Okay, we'll do it," said Shaneika. She grabbed my hand. "Thank you, Josiah."

"No problem," I assured, leaning on my cane. I was getting tired.

"I'll bring Ms. Todd's mother and boy out myself," said Goetz.

"Right," I responded. "See you later."

Asa placed my hand on her arm. "Sorry about butting in, but it is the best solution for everyone."

"It *is* the best thing. I'm sorry I couldn't think of it quick enough," I said, shaking my head.

"Well, let's go for a quick lunch and then I'll take you home to rest."

"That sounds good." I gave her arm a squeeze. "It's so good to see you even though it's for a short time."

"Yeah, I'm glad I came home too. Needed to take care of some things," she said, not looking at me.

Little did I know of what she was speaking and how it would affect me.

7

Anxious that I was going to have three houseguests, I called Jake's cell phone from the car. "That's funny," I remarked to Asa. "Jake's not answering. He usually picks up on the first ring."

Since she didn't comment, I thought nothing of it. When we arrived home, she had her driver let me out at the front door and followed. Again, Jake wasn't outside to meet me, which was his usual protocol. My heart started to pound faster as I now suspected something was wrong. I hurried to punch in the security code and unlock the first door to the bamboo entrance, pass the waterfall, and then the short pathway to the Butterfly's steel front doors where I had to punch in another code. Asa was right behind me.

"Jake. Jake!" I called when entering the house.

No one answered.

"Mom, I need to talk with you," said Asa.

Ignoring her, I fled to Jake's bedroom and flung open the door. It was empty. The closet door stood open showing a bare closet. I checked the bathroom. All his personal items were gone. I stood in the doorway, confused.

"Mother, we need to talk," demanded Asa, following me.

I turned to her. "What's going on? Where's Jake?"

My daughter led me to his bed, where we both sat down. She clasped my hands. "I reassigned him. Jake's gone and won't be back."

I couldn't hide the hurt from registering on my face. "But why? He was so good at his job. I still need his help."

"I know you're going to be mad, but I thought it best that he leave after seeing the two of you this morning."

I recoiled from her. "I think I am old enough to know if I want to kiss a man or not. What business it is of yours anyway?"

"I don't think it was just a simple kiss."

I abruptly stood up. "I don't need you to do that." I fled Jake's room.

Asa followed me into my bedroom. "Mom, you've got to listen. MOM – listen! Jake's married."

I whipped around. "I knew he was married. Jake told me."

"No. He's currently married. I would know. I make it a point to know what is going on in each of my employees' lives. He never got a divorce from his wife."

"That's not true," I denied. "He's divorced. He told me so. He was going to take me to a powwow to meet his family. I was going to meet his children."

Asa shook her head. "I'm sorry but I double checked this information."

Flabbergasted, I sat on the vanity seat. A kitten jumped on my shoulder and tried to climb on my head. I reach up and pulled him off. Looking in the mirror, I saw a stunned-looking woman with large green eyes staring back at me.

Asa continued. "You've just come into a large sum of money plus you own the Butterfly. Don't you see? My job is to protect you from everything, including men that might want to take advantage."

"Of a weak and vulnerable woman," I murmured. I watched as my reflection began to vanish in the mirror. I was losing myself.

"I'm so sorry, but Jake's been reassigned to another case. When the shock wears off, you'll see that it was for the best."

"So you think Jake was playing me?"

Asa thought for a moment, looking resigned as she spoke. "If he had really been serious, he would have told you the truth, letting the chips fall where they may." She kissed the top of my head. "I just couldn't stand by and let someone take advantage of you. Not on my watch."

"You've said that," I replied, trying to keep my tone neutral. "Don't worry about it, dear. It was just the heat of the moment. Nothing more than that on my side."

"Really? You looked at him like you were kind of in love."

"Tosh," I replied, patting her hand. "Nothing of the sort. Thank you for protecting me from making a fool of myself." I moved to the bed. "I am very tired now. Going to take a nap. Can you get the house ready for our guests?"

Looking relieved, Asa smiled. "I'll send for more food and make sure all the bed linens are fresh and the bathrooms are clean."

"Thank you, darling."

Asa blew me a kiss and closed my door.

I was grateful she left so she could not hear me sob into my pillow, where I shed a thousand tears. It was then I realized that I was never really going to send Jake away.

Never!

8

Lady Elsmere was getting into her Bentley when she spied Matt and myself seated comfortably in the back. "What's this?" she groused.

"I'm not going to let you go to the funeral by yourself," I replied, leaning forward, "and Matt's not going to let the two of us go alone. So it's both of us to keep you company on this awful day." I beckoned to her. "Come on."

Lady Elsmere turned to Charles, who nodded encouragingly. She gathered her mink coat about her and reluctantly got into the car. Then she sniffed as though smelling a stinkbug and acted put out. "Thank you," was all Lady Elsmere muttered until we reached the church.

Charles stopped in front of one of those small limestone Protestant churches that are little architectural gems that dot the Bluegrass landscape and beckon to the very rich and the very few. They house an elite club of worshipers – while the rest of us have to be content with large, impersonal churches, which look like concrete prisons from the outside. We also have a few that look like overgrown Quonset huts.

For some reason, church architects produce the most boring and least interesting buildings in town. They are devoid of any inspiration. Early twentieth-century, white clapboard churches with only one room are more beautiful than most of the contemporary places of worship in the Bluegrass, but then, that's just my opinion.

Matt scurried to open the car door, helping June and me out. Then he and I walked behind her going into the little stone church. I would have preferred sitting quietly in the back on one of the antique wooden pews, but June would have none of it. She strode to the front of the church, sitting in the family mourning section with Arthur's wife and family across the aisle. Trying to hide my embarrassment, I sank in my seat and buried my face in a battered hymnal. Matt just stared at the altar where the closed casket rested, trying not to flinch, as he knew the Greene family was looking at him, trying to place his relationship with the deceased. We were being upstarts, as we knew our proper place was more in the back, but June had to have her symbolic placement as part of the grieving family. I just hoped that June would hold her tongue until she got home.

The service was typical of Protestant funeral services. Psalm 23 was read – oh what a bore. Some nondescript hymns were sung and then bagpipes were played. For some reason, bagpipes make everyone misty-eyed. Strong beefy men, who use kindling for toothpicks, were suddenly reaching for their handkerchiefs to wipe their eyes, while sniffling women browsed in their purses for a tissue. God be praised, though – in thirty minutes the agony was over. Now just the trek to the cemetery.

We piled in our cars and followed the hearse to the stately Lexington Cemetery where our sacred dead lay buried next to the likes of Henry Clay, considered the greatest statesman of all time; Laura Clay, the first woman to run for president; John Hunt Morgan, the Thunderbolt of the Confederacy, who caused widespread damage to northern sympathizers' property; and Robert Todd, father to Mary Todd Lincoln and ancestral kin to Shaneika Mary Todd, whom was waiting with Detective Goetz.

Behind one of the forty-two varieties of trees in the garden cemetery, another cop discreetly took pictures of everyone attending. Shaneika and Goetz stood upon a small knoll watching the group congregate around a pile of earth and a frightening wound in the ground where we were going to deposit the earthly remains of Arthur Aaron Greene III for his final resting place. Another cop was taking down the license plate numbers of all the cars.

Matt and I both had our arms entwined with Lady Elsmere's, helping her walk the uneven ground, which I was having trouble traversing myself. We stood a respectful distance away from the casket and Arthur's family. The minister said a short prayer before someone stepped forward to sing "I'll Fly Away."

Suddenly June began trembling and moaning uncontrollably. Matt made comforting sounds to her, but her commotion was causing people to turn.

Charles ran up with a large black umbrella, which he used to help shield our noisy triangle. June pushed Matt away and fell into Charles' arms, which he folded around her, placing his rough cheek on her silver head leading her away. Matt and I followed.

It wasn't until Matt drove the Bentley out of the cemetery with Charles and June in the back, that I breathed again. I was shaking, reliving Brannon's death and now the pain of losing Jake.

"Why are you crying?" whispered Matt, leaning over.

I lied. "I always cry at funerals."

We did not speak again until Matt let Charles and June off at the front door and then parked the classic Bentley in the garage. He hurried me to his car and took me home to the Butterfly.

I could not stop weeping.

9

The next day I felt the bedcovers ripped off. It was hard to lift my head for my facial skin was sticking to the pillow. I did manage to open one swollen eye.

Franklin stood above, eyes aflamed, and arms akimbo. For some reason he looked ridiculous being all indignant towering over me. I chuckled.

"Oh, you think this is funny, do you?" hissed Franklin.

"Go away. You bother me, boy."

"Just when I think Matt and I are going to make it, you have to turn on the waterworks. All l heard last night is Josiah, Josiah, and June. I am so sick of you butting into our lives."

I managed to peel my skin off the pillowcase and face Franklin.

He took a step back. "Oh my goodness, you look terrible," cried Franklin, looking alarmed. "You're all lumpy." He started to laugh while sitting on the bed. "I guess the crying jag was an all-nighter from the looks of it. But still," he said, pointing a finger at me, "that doesn't excuse you for being a buttinsky."

"Franklin, I swear if I had a gun in my hand right now, I'd shoot you," I admonished. "Get the hell out of here and leave me alone, if you know what's good for you."

He poked my arm, which really pissed me off. "Where's Jake? He's usually around."

"Asa reassigned him."

"Really? I didn't think you were ready to let him go yet."

"O'nan is in jail and is being extradited. There wasn't any need for Jake, so she sent him on another assignment."

Franklin pondered this for a moment. "This wouldn't be the reason for all the tears, would it?"

"Of course not. Don't be ridiculous."

"Ahmmm. Well, it doesn't matter. You have a little boy as a houseguest who needs nurturing adults around him, not hysterical pain pill addicts. Pull yourself together, woman. People need you." He slapped me on the fanny. "Get up. I'll make your bed while you get ready and tell ole granny out there to make you some breakfast. We're going sleuthing."

To emphasize Franklin's argument, Baby thumped his huge head down on the bed next to mine, licked his nose and belched. Then he made a noise, which I swear was "get up" in doggy language. I couldn't fight the two of them, so I arose from my bed of self-loathing and got cracking.

When I sat at the breakfast table, Shaneika's mother, Mrs. Todd, slapped down two eggs over easy, country fried ham, hash browns smothered with cheese, and buttered grits on the side followed by a glass of cold milk. And scratch biscuits!

Did I mention the scratch biscuits were light and fluffy and smothered with gravy made from skillet drippings!

All the good stuff Jake never let me eat. It was heaven. Mrs. Todd, not trusting my cooking utensils, had brought her prized cast iron skillets.

Eunice Leticia Mary Todd was everything that I was not. Like Shaneika, her skin was a light caramel color with fine features and pronounced almond-shaped eyes. She was just a decade older but unlike me, she took pride in her appearance still. Her speech was measured as she thought before she spoke. Her hair and makeup were carefully tended to and her dress was an ironed cotton print accentuated at the waist with a pretty braided belt. She reminded me of a black Donna Reed. All she needed was the pearl necklace. And man oh man, could that woman cook. Old fashioned southern cooking with bacon drippings, fresh cream, butter, and lard.

I loved her.

After breakfast, I felt better and waddled to Franklin's Smart Car. Going north on Tates Creek, we passed Taylor Made Farm, which was originally created to board mares being bred with Gainesway Farm stallions. Gainesway Farm was backed by Gaines dog food fortune.

Farther north is Overbrook Farm, founded by W.T. Young, who made Big Top peanut butter, later known as

Jif. I now pass Overbrook Farm with trepidation, wondering if the future holds its fate to be another cookie-cutter housing ghetto.

We cut over Man O' War Boulevard and found ourselves shortly on the east side of the county. Straddling both Fayette and Clark County boundaries, we turned into Royal Blue Stables.

Stopping the car, Franklin reached over me and pushed open my door. "Go do what you do best," he said. "Irritate people. I'll wait here, plotting my next move to get Matt off your wretched farm."

"It's a gift, Franklin. It's a gift." I climbed out of the car with my wolf head cane, which Franklin had purchased for me in Key West, and walked into the barn. Though I walked much better, my limp was still noticeable and I brushed my hair over my hearing aid. Other than that, I looked pretty perky for a gal my age. I even had a little style since Franklin insisted on picking out my clothes. I had to admit he did have a certain flair.

I rounded the barn and made for the place where Arthur had been killed. I would recognize it from the police photos Shaneika had shown me. I didn't ask how she got them.

Passed by several illegal employees who waved but never bothered to ask me who I was. They feared that I might be an INS agent. I soon found myself by Comanche's empty stall. There was a ratty fold-up chair in the corner, which I pulled out and sat in the doorway of the stall, looking around. Occasionally, I poked the straw with my cane while inhaling the smell of manure, hay, oats, leather, saddle soap, and horse sweat. It smelled like the earth – natural and sweet – but the barn was a mess with hay bales stacked here and there, buckets strewn about. This was not how a horse barn was supposed to look. Obviously this was a third-rate establishment, but even so I thought it unusually dirty. Most horse barns are cleaner than people's houses. Maybe Shaneika was running out of money chasing after her dream.

I turned over my notebook, looking at my scribbling.

In Lincoln's story, Comanche had started to make a commotion, which woke him up. I turned and looked at the little hay bed Lincoln had made near the outside wall.

Comanche had been nervous and hard to handle that day so Lincoln had volunteered to stay, hoping to calm him down for training the next day. Shaneika agreed as there was a watchman on duty all night and the rest of the hands went home after seven. Shaneika had left Lincoln at 10:30 p.m. and would be back at 4 a.m. to get Comanche ready for his early morning training. Lincoln had his cell phone and the night watchman agreed to keep tabs on the boy, saying he never left his post.

But he did that night.

The watchman had forgotten his lunch and went down the road to get some food before McDonald's closed. He had left Lincoln alone for thirty-five minutes. When he returned, he discovered Arthur Greene hanging from one of the barn's beams and Lincoln unconscious on the floor.

I dragged the chair with me as I followed Linc's story.
I turned the corner where he said he had seen the two
men arguing. A horse reached out from his stall and
nipped my shoulder. Finding oats by his stall, I let him
eat some from my hand and then rubbed his muzzle.
"Can you tell me anything?" I asked. "Did you see
anything, big boy? Yes? No?"

The stallion tossed his head as if to say no and returned
to munching hay, ignoring me.

Putting the chair by the wall where Lincoln said he hid,
I looked out and studied the area. From where Lincoln
had hunkered down, it would indeed be hard to make
out the two men but easy enough to listen as sound
echoed off the concrete walls. I studied the hay pulley
used to hoist Arthur's body up to the rafters. Why not
just leave the dead man on the floor? Why hoist him up?
Was that a symbolic gesture?

Poking the dirt around the area where Lincoln had
fallen, I noticed something glimmer near a stall. I pulled
the chair over to its location and sat, digging with my
cane. Out popped a gold fountain pen encrusted with
dirt. Dragging it over with my cane, I was about to pick it
up when a tall, powerfully built man came through the
archway, and upon spying me, walked towards my chair.
"Can I help you?" he asked politely, but I could tell his
smile was hard-set. I instinctively stepped on the pen,
thus hiding it.

"I'm Mrs. Reynolds. I'm an investor in Comanche,
Shaneika Todd's horse."

"Yeah?"

"I thought I'd come to see where all the commotion took place. Try to make sense of it all."

"You're not a reporter or anything?"

Surprised, I answered, "No, I own the Butterfly next to Lady Elsmere's farm on Tates Creek." I thought everyone in Lexington knew who I was.

"Ahh," he replied, not impressed at all. He pointed to one of the rafters. "That's where Mr. Greene was found. It sure shook me up."

"Have any idea who killed him?"

"All rich men have enemies and the horse business naturally brews jealousy."

"Like who?"

"Not going to name names but you can ask around. Somebody will talk to you but it won't be me."

"And who might you be?"

"Dan Slade. I'm farm manager here."

I shook his hand, which felt clammy. I noticed he was wearing an antique Masonic ring.

"What about close friends?"

Slade tugged at his Lexington Legends baseball cap. "You might try Aspen Lancaster. He was Greene's breeder and had been with him for years. They were in college together and part of the Thin Thirty. If anyone knew him, Lancaster knew, but he won't talk to you."

"Why?"

"Why should he?" retorted Mr. Slade, who then abruptly walked away.

"Hey," I yelled after him. "What's the Thin Thirty?"

"One of Lexington's dirty little secrets."

"Tell me."
"Find out yourself."
Well – Jumping Jehosaphat!

10

Lexington is still divided into a southern social class system. It's a little more blended and harder to see, but very much in existence. At the apex of this pyramid is the horse aristocracy, which is resented by those who don't understand Kentucky's horse industry and its economic impact. This resentment can be sensed every time the horse industry goes to the Kentucky legislature to get something passed to help their industry, like slot machines at the horse tracks.

The horse industry rightly argues that gambling money is flowing like water out of Kentucky to Indiana and Ohio, states that have expanded the confines of sinful gambling, thus hurting the kingly sport of horse racing.

Also rightly, they argue that without the horse and bourbon industries, Kentucky would lose what little prestige and glamour it has left. Tobacco is dead. Hemp has been outlawed and Kentucky's wine industry, which was once number one in the country, never recovered from the Prohibition Era. Now the only thing that Kentucky is number one in is domestic situations that result in the killing of children.

The average Joe argues back that he is taxed through the nose to pay for the overloaded health care and education systems for the families of the migrant workers the horse industry brings in. Citizens claim they get stuck with the bill when migrant workers don't have health insurance.

Most of the people living in the Bluegrass were not born to it and don't understand its history or culture. They don't give a damn about the Thoroughbred or Standardbred industries, hate the smell of horse manure, and think the horse farms should be plowed under. They have never ridden a horse. All they know is that horses have nothing to do with them . . . or so they think. They don't know that horses are the lifeblood of the Bluegrass – the very thing that makes Kentucky unique and like no other place on earth.

The horse industry argues back that it drops a bundle into Kentucky's economy by attracting tourists who spend money on hotels, food, wine, liquor, restaurants, and sightseeing. The horse farms also spend a fortune on cars, trucks, horse trailers, gas, stable maintenance, antebellum mansion maintenance, and insurance.

There are also signs, vehicle maintenance, hay, straw, grain, oats, trees, landscaping, horse equipment like saddles, silks, and boots, garden tools, grass seed, vets, farriers, lumber, posts, wire for wooden fences, paint, masons for rock fences, trainers, jockeys, breeders, grooms, support staff like secretaries, receptionists, accountants, lawyers, caterers, office equipment, office furniture and so on.

The equine aristocrats also bestow gifts like the Lucille Parker Markey Cancer Center, which is a world-renowned cancer treatment facility, or the W.T. Young library at UK. Keeneland Race Course, a non-profit racetrack, has given millions to local charities and is remembered for paying to have at-risk children inoculated with the Salk vaccine, helping to wipe out polio in the fifties.

The real truth is that most people in the horse business are regular working joes that help keep Kentucky's economy going. A horse farm might employee 150 people while a cattle farm might offer three jobs. And the migrant workers are needed because Kentuckians will no longer do the work that these farms require.

And so the arguments go round and round while the resentment between the classes builds up.

I was thinking about all of this as Franklin sped towards Lady Elsmere's farm. I knew that Arthur and June had shared Aspen Lancaster as a breeder for both farms had breeding sheds. I called Charles, who told me that Aspen was at the farm now as he was doing the last of the scheduled breedings for the year.

"Put the pedal to the metal," I told Franklin, who sped down Tates Creek Road. We made Lady Elsmere's farm in record time and Franklin followed the path to the breeding shed, where he dropped me off. He had seen a horse being bred before and did not want to witness a repeat performance.

I must admit Thoroughbred horse breeding is not for the squeamish. All Thoroughbreds must be bred through what those in the business call "live cover" with witnesses in attendance.

I entered the breeding shed by the side door and took a seat by June, who tried to observe most of the matings. She was taking notes and giving instructions to her farm manager.

"What are you doing here?" she asked, surprised.

"Which one is Aspen Lancaster?"

She pointed to a large man who was wearing a helmet and padding preparing a mare for mating. "What do you want with him?"

"I was told that he knew Arthur better than anyone. I wanted to ask him some questions."

June excused her farm manager. "They go back a long way," June confirmed. "They were roommates at UK back in the early sixties, but I never felt they were especially close for the past several years."

"Any reason why not?"

"Well, they started out as equals and then Arthur shot ahead financially. I think it galled Aspen to work for him, though he never demonstrated any hard feelings. Just something I felt."

I watched Aspen put padded shields on the mare's withers and neck, as some stallions were predisposed to bite and kick. Another member of the breeding team wrapped the tail in gauze while another checked the vulva for possible disease. Then the mare's upper lip was twisted into a knot with a long stick called a twitch, which kept the mare under control so she wouldn't buck forward. All handlers gave the thumbs-up to Aspen, who gave orders for the stallion to enter.

An entryway handler took his place near the rear of the mare. He was to guide the stallion's penis into the mare for quick and efficient breeding. A brute of a horse was brought in, neighing and tossing his head. The stallion mounted the mare without incident with the video camera rolling. The noisy and violent affair was over in minutes. The stallion was led out as the mare was checked over for any injury and then led to another barn.

"Who's the mare?"

"My Lady Elizabeth. She is going to give me a Kentucky Derby winner. I've never won the Kentucky Derby, but I'm going to before I die."

The thought that she had better hurry entered my mind, but I shook it off. "Do you want me to ask Aspen questions or do you want just to forget about Arthur's death?"

"Ask away. I have no strong feeling for Aspen. I only hired him as Arthur suggested him as a good breeding man."

June got up to leave.

"One more thing, June. What does the Thin Thirty refer to?"

June's lips tightened. "Oh my, I haven't heard that term in decades. It refers to the 1962 UK football team.

I think it was Larry Boeck from the *Courier-Journal* that
gave the team that name."

"Why?"

June looked uneasy and I could tell she was debating
on how much to tell me. "UK had hired Charlie
Bradshaw as the new coach and his methods were . . .
well, they were extreme. The football team went down
from 88 players to just 30 in a matter of months and the
remaining players were so thin, they were dubbed the
Thin Thirty."

"What did this coach do?"

"You'll have to ask Aspen. He was on the team with
Arthur. It must have been horrible because Arthur got
the shakes when he was reminded of 1962. He told me
being on that team was pure hell but he wouldn't give me
any details. You'll have to talk to Aspen about that," she
repeated before she flew out the door.

That was the first of many evasions I would get about
the Thin Thirty. Like I said before, the past is never dead
in Lexington. It is not even past. And before I was
finished, I would be revealing secrets that people had
buried for over fifty years and wished had stayed deep in
the ground.

June sent word to Aspen Lancaster that I wanted to
talk with him after he was finished. He made me wait
forty-five minutes while he finished the documentation
on the breeding. Finally Aspen made his way to where I
was seated.

He was wearing khaki pants with a plaid cotton shirt that strained at the waistline. "You need to talk with me?" he asked curtly.

Immediately my "bullshit antenna" went on. I have always found that when people are brisk and rude, they are usually hiding something.

Of course, Jake would disagree with me. He maintained they just didn't want to speak with me.

Who would not want to speak with me?

"Yes, Mr. Lancaster. I'm Mrs. Reynolds. I own the farm next door."

He said nothing, staring at me.

"Would you like to sit down? I want to ask you a few questions about Mr. Greene, if you don't mind?"

"Are you a cop?"

"Well no, but I own part-interest in Comanche, who was at the Royal Blue Stables when Mr. Greene was murdered."

"So you don't have a warrant or anything like that? I don't really have to talk with you?"

"Why would you not want to?"

"Because I don't want to speak with gossipy busybodies who've got no business sticking their noses into what was a suicide of a dear friend."

I guffawed – suicide. "Oh, come now. How could that man strangle himself and then hoist his dead body up to the rafters?"

"Stranger things have happened."

"Strange, but not possible. Surely you can spare me a few minutes?"

"Nope, don't think I can." He turned and started out of the room.

"What is the Thin Thirty to you, Mr. Lancaster?"

Aspen stopped dead in his tracks. Turning towards me, he hissed, "the most goddamn worst year of my life. Now excuse me. I've got work to do."

Then he was gone like a puff of smoke.

11

The next day was Saturday and I was in my booth at the Farmers' Market. It was the pinnacle of Kentucky's harvest season with both the summer and fall vegetables coming in. The booth spaces were going to be tight and hard to negotiate since most of the farmers would be attending. And the place would be packed with customers since the corn farmers were attending with trucks full of Silver Queen corn. Corn was a huge draw.

I would need help. Since Jake was no longer around, I had to coax one of Charles' grandsons. Lincoln tagged along, but his cheerful chirping was getting on my nerves. I sent him along to help my friend, Irene Meckler, who actually liked children. She promised she and her husband, Jefferson Davis Meckler, would keep a close eye on him.

I was of the W.C. Fields' school concerning children. "How do you like children, Mr. Fields?"

"Parboiled," he replied.

Around 1 p.m., I had sold out of my clover honey. Kentucky makes over thirty different honeys while the United States makes over three hundred. Our bees make clover, wildflower, sourwood, buckwheat, alfalfa, tulip poplar, and locust honey, just to mention a few. Our honey color ranges from clear to black, depending on the nectar of the plant harvested by the honeybees. Kentucky produces some of the finest honey in the nation – all from the 4,000 hives we have in the state.

I told Charles' grandson to pay my booth fee to the Market Manager and pack up. I was going to the public library on Main Street to do some research. He could pick me up there. Since the library was only a block away, I managed it fine. I was relieved to find a spare computer that I did not have to wrestle away from one of the many transients who call the library their "day home."

I typed in "Thin Thirty."

Nothing.

Then I typed in Charlie Bradshaw and got lots of material. After a quick reading of articles, it seemed like Charlie Bradshaw, a Bear Bryant devotee, was a good Christian man who was never in a scandal concerning women, drugs or gambling. Seemed like he had kept his nose clean during his career. So what was the problem?

I thought back to Lincoln's statement. He said one of the men cried, 'You can't tell. It would ruin me."

Both Aspen and Arthur had served on the 1962 football team and both had been reluctant to talk about it. Was there a connection between this and Arthur's death? Why were Arthur's pockets filled with rocks? What was the message in that? And the curious bucket of water? And why did Kelly tell me to look for the widow's son?

Charles' grandson picked me up in front of the library. Lincoln was bouncing up and down in the back. Apparently Irene had fed Lincoln treats that contained a lot of sugar. Thanks, Irene.

Lincoln's constant chatter even got on the nerves of the grandson, who raced down Tates Creek Road. I was home within minutes and gratefully gave Lincoln over to his grandmother.

Shaneika was sunning by the pool in a stunning bikini. She had just had a lunch of pinto beans and cornbread swathed in butter and washed down by sweet raspberry iced tea. She was now spooning in some hot apple cinnamon crumble pie à la mode. Shaneika looked like a purring sleek panther.

I hungrily peered into the empty dishes.

She lifted her sunglasses to see who cast a shadow over her. "You know I could get used to this," she yawned.

I sat down at the table and glanced at the pool. It didn't look as clean as when Jake had lived here. There were leaves in the water. In fact, nothing looked as bright and shiny as when Jake lived here. I was beginning to realize all that he had done.

I would need staff once Shaneika and her family returned to their respective homes. I couldn't cope with the Butterfly on my own. The thought of this beautiful house being empty once more gave me a sad feeling. No. It was more like loneliness.

Mrs. Todd brought out a lunch tray, identical to what Shaneika had eaten, for me plus an iced tea for herself.

"You didn't have to do that," I lied, mentally licking my chops as I inhaled the steaming bowl of beans.

"Don't mind. Makes me feel needed." She replied, sitting down beside me in the shade, sipping on her tea. "Love this view. You can see for miles. We must be way up."

"Mom, don't remind Josiah of the cliff."

"I'm sorry, honey. Did I bring back bad memories?"

I sprinkled fresh-cut onions over the beans after giving them a heavy dose of salt and pepper. "I'm so over it. Get tired of talking about my "accident.""

Shaneika snorted. "Is that what you call it?"

"Well, how do you want me to refer to it? My attempted murder?" I snapped.

"Girls," warned Mrs. Todd.

The glass door slid open and Lincoln hopped out in a Spider-Man bathing suit munching on a peanut butter sandwich followed by Baby and a swarm of kittens. To get away from Baby's annoying attempts to cash in on the sandwich, Lincoln sat in the shallow water on the pool steps. Baby didn't like water; nor did the cats, which were prowling along the poolside keeping a watchful eye on Lincoln.

"I hope you cleaned up after yourself," called Mrs. Todd.

Lincoln shrugged while joyfully stuffing the rest of the sandwich into his mouth. There was a great deal of peanut butter on his face, which I hoped would not get into the pool. It would play havoc with the water filter.

Thankfully, Shaneika strode over and wiped the goo off Lincoln's face. He jumped playfully in the water as Shaneika sat on the pool ledge watching him.

After dispatching half of the beans, I came up for air. "Mrs. Todd, do you remember anything about the UK 1962 football year? Any talk about it?"

"That's when only white boys played on the team."

"Any of those boys stand out in your mind – something odd?"

"Nothing odd but the coaching staff."

"In what way?"

"At the time, nothing was done about it. It was how we pushed our boys to be men. Things were rougher then than now."

"Nothing was done about what?"

"Well, things that went on then were considered perfectly normal but now . . . nobody would stand for it. Nobody."

"Mrs. Todd, please tell me. What was odd?"

"For one thing the coach was known for not giving the team water during practice."

"What? That's outrageous."

"Today we say it's outrageous. Back then it was building character."

Shaneika interrupted, "Some coaches still do that today. They ought to be sued."

"What else?"

"There were rumors of rough treatment if the players didn't do well in practice. They claimed that the staff hit them sometimes breaking their teeth or that they were humiliated before the team. Others say players lost too much weight, forty, sometimes fifty pounds."

"Is that why the team was called the Thin Thirty?"

"Yes. Then the boys' scholarships were taken away from whoever was either booted off or had quit the team in protest. The players claimed that Bradshaw was gunning for them, forcing them to sign away their scholarships."

"And nobody stopped this?"

"Finally the NCAA suspended UK from the post-season play in 1964 because of the scholarship issue and the fact Bradshaw had been conducting illegal winter training. But Bradshaw wasn't doing anything that some other coaches weren't doing at the time. And UK would do anything for a winning team."

"Was it a winning team?"

"It was a draw. Bradshaw resigned and went on to Troy State University, having a good reputation there. I know all this as my husband and his father were football fanatics. We always went to the UK home games. In fact, one of our boys played for UK football for several years before he busted his shoulder."

"And he never received real monetary compensation for his loss. Colleges make big money off these boys as if they were professional athletes and then throw them aside if they get hurt without paying true penalties. Many of these players don't even graduate with a degree. It is absolutely shameful how colleges treat their athletes," spat out Shaneika.

I ate a spoonful of beans – thinking.

"Then there was that sex scandal that was hushed up."

The spoon fell out of my mouth.

"What sex scandal?"

"Almost no ones knows about it now," Mrs. Todd commented.

"Mrs. Todd, I'm gonna bust a gut if you don't spill the beans," I whined.

"I don't like to talk about such things. I only know this because my husband's cousin has a friend who was a domestic at the house of those two men who came in the late fifties. They bought a big house on Lakewood Drive and began having parties for all of the college athletes, paying special attention to football teams."

"Two men as in business partners or as in something else?"

"Well, I don't rightly know, but I can call Jimmy and see if his friend is still alive, so you can talk to him."

My eyes must have popped out of my head. "Can you call right now?" I asked.

Mrs. Todd looked at me with surprise.

"Please. This football connection is the only lead I have for Mr. Greene's murder. Nothing else is on radar."

Mrs. Todd shot a quick glance at Lincoln and rose from her seat. "Yes, I'll call right this very moment," and she went inside the house.

I finished the beans and drank my tea.

Giving the bowl to Baby, he licked it clean. He showed his appreciation by burrowing his snout into my crotch so I could rub his ears before he returned his attention to Lincoln. He seemed fascinated by the boy and followed him everywhere. Perhaps Baby thought of Lincoln as a pet. Who knows what wild fantasies went on in that dog's head?

Finally, Mrs. Todd returned to the patio wearing a bemused smile. "We are to meet with my cousin's friend tonight at his house. The man is ill, so he can't leave but he will be happy to talk with us."

"That's great," I said, before excusing myself. I went to telephone June to see if she had any pictures of Arthur and Aspen when younger. She did and we were to pick them up as we left for Nicholasville, where the interviewee lived. Happily I put down the phone and checked the clock. I had just enough time to take a nap before we left.

12

Several hours later Mrs. Todd and I arrived at the home of her husband's cousin, Jimmy. He met us at the door with keys in hand and escorted us several doors down. Using a spare key, he ushered us to a small one-level house. "Hey Leon, we're here," he called, showing us into a cozy living room lit with a gas log fire even though it was warm outside.

Sitting in a worn green recliner was Leon Short, an ancient grizzled man attached to an oxygen tank. He waved us to sit down on a worn corduroy couch while Jimmy helped him sit up and take off his mask.

"Jimmy, get these fine women some Coca-Cola," rasped Leon. He waved away our collective no's. "Get me one too. Lots of ice." He rearranged a crocheted afghan around his legs, looking at us expectantly. "It's been a long time since I had lady visitors. Very nice. Very nice. Jimmy says you want to talk to me about some

81

white men I worked for in the early sixties. That was a long time ago. What do you want to know?"

I leaned forward to accept a glass from Jimmy. "I want to ask about some rumors I've heard. About two men who came into town and were interested in male athletes."

Leon smiled. "The Lord says that the truth can never be hidden. I guess he's right. You're talking about two men who came to our fair city in the late fifties – Mr. Lonnie and Mr. Jim. They were wrestling promoters and came with buckets full of money to spread around."

"To spread around for what purpose?" I asked.

"Allegedly for some tender southern white-meat chicken," Leon chuckled.

I looked at Mrs. Todd, bewildered.

She just shook her head.

Jimmy twittered nervously and interceded on our behalf. "Behave now, Leon. Mrs. Todd is a regular church-going woman and I don't think Mrs. Reynolds is used to rough talk either."

"My apologies, ladies. Like I said, I'm not used to female companionship, at least, in a long time." Leon coughed into a handkerchief. "You ever heard rumors about Rock Hudson coming to Lexington?"

"Yes, when I first came here, people would say that Rock Hudson was in town," I responded.

"He came here to visit Elizabeth Taylor when she was filming *Raintree County* and liked it so much that he came often. Now why would a big star like that come to our little country town so often? Don't know? Let me explain it to y'all. Lexington in those days was filthy rich; horses and tobacco was king. But Lexington was also a little cosmopolitan island in a redneck southern world. There were a lot of smart people in Lexington those days due to IBM, Transylvania, and UK, who believed in minding their own business. Where else could Henry Faulkner and Sweet Evening Breeze go prancing around without gettin' beat up all the time? There were some altercations, but for the most part Lexington was a very tolerant place for its "eccentrics." As long as people didn't come right out and talk about certain things, nothing was said. You might say Lexington was protective."

I took a sip of my drink, not taking my eyes off Leon, who was enjoying being the center of attention.

"Now I am setting up what Lexington was like. Famous people like Tennessee Williams and big movie stars flying in all the time to go to parties. Those were the days when people socialized more. Everyone was having picnics, throwing parties, giving barbeques. People spent the evenings on their porches, going to other people's houses for dinner or out to dance all the time. Even on weeknights, downtown was packed with folks. People got out. They didn't stay home watching their TV like they do now. Lexington was a very social town.

"It was in this atmosphere that I went to work for two men who lived on Lakewood Drive. It wasn't long before I knew what they were."

"Hustlers?"

"Much, much more." Leon paused for dramatic effect. "Mrs. Reynolds, they were predators, sure and simple. They preyed on young men. They liked them fresh off the farm and Lexington was their hunting ground."

"How would they prey on them?" asked Mrs. Todd, alarmed.

"I can only tell you what I saw. They'd throw these lavish parties with starlets from Hollywood, using them as bait. There was always lots of food washed down with liquor and they showed dirty movies in the basement. Then they'd get these boys drunk and take advantage of them. If that didn't work, they used money to coax the boys or gave them expensive gifts."

"I don't understand how you can make a heterosexual man do homosexual acts if he's not," said Mrs. Todd.

"If you're poor or young, you can be coaxed to do anything. Besides, at their age of 18, 19, 20, you can manipulate young'uns to do lots of stuff they wouldn't do when older and more mature. These guys were promoters and good at getting people to do what they wanted."

"You actually saw them have sex with these boys?"

"No ma'am, but what could they have been doing behind locked doors and those boys comin' out looking all embarrassed and sheepish."

"How does that play into the Thin Thirty?"

"Their specialty was the very young football players, but the sex was a sideline. I think the gambling was more important."

"Gambling?" I echoed.

"Like I said, my bosses were wrestling promoters, so they had strong connections in big cities like Chicago and Atlanta. There were rumors in the black community that they had started taking orders to rig college games."

I held my breath.

Leon wheezed, "They get players to really bump up the point spread and then get them to lose a important game." He took a sip of his Coca-Cola and closed his eyes.

"UK has been investigated in the past for gambling in basketball, but I've never heard of this," I replied.

"Like I said, no investigation was done," Leon mumbled, slowing down like a worn out record.

A sound escaped from my nose that sounded like snorting, a noise of disbelief.

Leon sat with his eyes closed.

I wondered if he had fallen asleep and glanced at Mrs. Todd. She shook his knee.

Stirring, Leon almost dropped his glass. "Sorry. Just taking a little rest." He rubbed his grizzled cheek.

"So what happened?"

"Some of the older players squealed to Coach Bradshaw about what was going on. Coach Bradshaw was not going to let his boys be taken advantage of like that. Supposedly the boys in black and white paid my employers a visit. Feeling the chill, my bosses left town within a week."

"Cops?"

"You bet."

"What did you think of these men?"

"They paid me good money, way above the pay grade at that time. I guess it was hush money but they never bothered me. I was the wrong color," chuckled Leon. "You've got to understand how things were in 1962. There was white man's business and black man's business. This was white man's doings. I just kept my mouth shut and cashed my paycheck."

"What about Rock Hudson?"

"Rock Hudson was Rock Hudson. I heard he liked going to the Gilded Cage. I never saw him do nothing but drink and talk to the boys. If he did more, I never saw it, but I heard stories, especially of one local boy he helped become a TV star in Hollywood."

I handed him pictures that June had given to me of Arthur Greene and Aspen Lancaster. "Do you recognize these men being at the house on Lakewood Drive? Of course, they're years older in these pictures."

Leon got out his reading glasses and carefully perused the photographs. "Sure, I recognize 'em." He pointed to one of the men, "This here is Arthur Greene." He pointed to the other person. "That boy is Mr. Arthur's best friend, Aspen Lancaster. They were regulars at the house."

"No doubt?"

"I'll swear on the Bible."

"Would you be willing to make a legal affidavit?"

"Everyone involved is dead or near-dead. Whatcha want with this information?"

"I want to right a wrong and help a young boy."

"Save a boy from being wronged?"

"Yes. Her grandson," I replied, pointing to Mrs. Todd.

Leon studied Mrs. Todd and then said, "I'll be here when you need me. I might even have some old pictures in boxes somewhere. I'll have my daughter look."

I turned to Mrs. Todd. "I think we just found our connection to Lincoln."

13

I gave Shaneika several family albums with photographs of Arthur Greene at different ages inserted throughout. She was casually going to go through them with Lincoln and see if he recognized anyone.

Since I didn't need to be there, I drove to Frankfort to see a good buddy of mine, Clay, who owned a bee supply business. I needed some wax inserts for super frames and replacement hive bodies. The place was packed with other beekeepers wanting their orders filled, so Clay waved me into his office to wait.

I limped into his office and hung my cane up on the coat rack. I was still not used to driving long distances and my left leg was beginning to throb and my hearing aid was about to slip off. After adjusting the hearing aid, I put my feet up on some boxes to rest. Leaning back in the plump office chair, I spied Clay and his staff busily satisfying customers. Knowing this was going to take a long time, I settled into my seat and began nosing around Clay's desk.

I know this is a bad habit. I know it's rude, but it's amazing what you can find out about people just by poking around their desk or bathroom cabinet. Yes, I'm that kind of person who would read an unlocked diary, which is why I don't keep one. And I had nothing else to do but snoop.

After going through his mail, which consisted of business matters – no juicy love letters – I studied the pictures on his walls. It seemed that Clay was a softball player in his younger days. I noticed several other beekeepers I knew including my friend, Larry Bingham. The date on the last picture of Clay and Larry together was ten years ago. Hmmm.

I must have dozed off because the next thing I knew Clay was pulling on my shoe. Rubbing my eyes, I sat up. "Sorry, I fell asleep."

"I've loaded everything up for you," announced Clay, who obviously wanted his comfy chair, but I was not ready to give it up yet. He handed me an invoice.

"Busy day, huh?" I asked.

"Been running my tail off," he said, "but that's a good problem to have."

"Yeah," I said, reluctantly motioning to Clay to help me up. I got up on my two legs and Clay handed me my cane. He looked worn out and seemed relieved that he could sit in his own chair.

"Hey, Clay?"

"Hey what," he returned, giving me a series of quick looks. "Josiah, did you go though my mail? Everything is out of order."

"Of course not," I pouted, acting put out. Wanting to change the subject, I said, "I didn't know that you played softball."

Clay glanced at the pictures. "Yeah, we had a great team. I played shortstop."

"I noticed Larry played too."

"He played left field, but then he got too old to play. Anyway that's what he said. Stopped playing after our last big Bluegrass Stakes game. Aw, that was some game."

"You still play?"

Clay gave me a big grin. "Naw, got too many things going on now. Don't have the time, but wish I did. Lots of fun."

He walked me out to the car, holding my cane while I struggled to get in. Clay tossed the cane in the back seat. "Bees doing OK?"

"The best I can tell, but I am going to need help this next harvest, which is coming up very soon. Know anybody that can help?"

"If you can't find anyone, give me a call. I'll help you," replied Clay.

"Maybe I'll ask Larry again," I said. "I just hate to bother him all the time."

"He doesn't mind. But seriously, call me if you can't find anyone."

"Thanks, Clay."

He patted the roof of my car before saying, "Be careful, Josiah."

I waved goodbye.

Since I would pass Larry's house on the way home, I decided to drop by and see if he was available for the summer's honey harvest. Within twenty-five minutes I was pulling up into his driveway. At the front of the driveway was Larry's honey stand where jars of golden honey were stacked alongside a cigar box. People paid on the honor system and it was amazing that honey or money were rarely stolen. Perhaps it was because everyone knew that Larry was a retired G-man.

Underneath his love of classic rock 'n' roll, puzzles, and 1940's era slang was someone who was not to be trifled with. Maybe it was his eyes. They seemed to tear a person up.

I pulled up next to his fancy honey house and honked my horn. Larry shambled out. I smiled and called his name, but I swear for the briefest of seconds a shadow pass over his face. His eyes narrowed. It startled me, but then he smiled.

"Hey, Toots. Whatcha doing?" he inquired in a friendly voice.

I must have been imagining his dismay upon seeing me. I shook it off.

"Came for a quick chin wag. Just got back from Clay's. Clay said if you can't help me with the next harvest, he would do it."

"And get some of the best honey in the area as a reward! I should say not. Deal as before. I get a fourth of the harvest."

"That takes a load off my mind."

"Now, I'm just going to harvest the hives. I'm not going to work the bees for you."

"Okay. That's my problem. I'll sort it out."

"Why don't you go into my office and cool your heels. There are some drinks in a cooler. I'm going get you some fresh tomatoes and squash from my garden. Only be a minute."

"That sounds great, Larry. Thanks."

I hobbled into the honey house and sat at Larry's desk, as there wasn't another suitable chair.

Uh oh. It wasn't two seconds before I was lifting up old bee magazines and playing with broken bee equipment thrown on the top of his old desk. I moved some letters so I could glance at his desk calendar. My, oh my, he was a very busy guy. Gave talks at a lot of bee clubs. Various doctor appointments.

While perusing, I knocked over some broken frames Larry had been repairing. Bending down, my elbow pushed the desk calendar out of place. Stuck in between paper folds of the calendar were several postcards.

Pulling one out, I wondered whom it was from. On the front was a picture of the southwest desert. I flipped it over, though feeling a wee bit guilty. On the back was a short note from a friend saying that the hunting was great and wished Larry would join him. Signed Tom.

I caught my breath as I studied the word Tom. A distinctive hook on the bottom of the T rang a bell, and I realized that this was the handwriting of Tellie Pidgeon.

Tellie Pidgeon tried to frame me for murdering her husband, Richard Pidgeon, and she almost succeeded. She left Kentucky with my blessing, but not before I got her confession on tape and blackmailed her into giving me her Prius and money.

I know. I know. I'm bad sometimes.

There was no return address, but the card had been mailed to Larry at a private post office box.

Hearing Larry round the corner, I pushed the postcard into my pocket and straightened the desk.

"Hey, no drinks yet?"

"Waiting for you, good buddy," I said, trying to keep my face from sinking. "Oh by the way, where's the noble consort Brenda?"

Larry hesitated for a split second. "Went to see her mother. She's getting up there you know."

"No, I didn't, but send Brenda my regards when you talk to her."

"Sure."

"Well, I've got to be going. Thanks for the vegetables, Larry. I'm going to slice them up tonight."

"Anything for you."

He walked out with me to the Prius. I couldn't wait to get away, but took my time chatting about people we both knew. Finally I started the car and turned around. Looking in the mirror, I caught him staring at the honey house and then at me.

I got the hell out of there.

Flying home like my Prius had wings, I was thankful to see that Goetz still had a cop car at the entrance to my driveway. I waved to the guy, pulling up alongside him.

"Anything unusual?" I asked.

"Very quiet, ma'am."

"That's good," I said, handing him Larry's vegetables.

"Gee, thanks," he cooed happily, putting them down on the seat beside him.

"Do me a favor, will ya?" I asked.

The policeman nodded.

"Let me know if you see a midnight blue Ford Explorer cruising by. In it will be a white male in his late sixties with frosty blue eyes. Sorta like Paul Newman's eyes. Jessamine County license plates. I'd really appreciate it."

"Something I should know about?"

"Too soon to tell. Just a hunch."

"Okay. I'll be on the lookout."

"What's your name?"

"Jeremy Snow."

"You'll let me know?"

"Yes, ma'am."

"Thank you. Much obliged."

"Just one thing," requested the young policeman. "Who's Paul Newman?"

I groaned and started down the gravel driveway, thinking I had to be wrong. But if I was right, I had to move fast. Stopping the car by the front gate, I punched in the code to the bamboo door, hurried past the waterfall and punched in another code to the steel front doors. Hearing the beep, I threw one of the double doors open and ran to my room as fast as my limp would allow me. Once inside I locked the bedroom door and dragged a chair over by the floor safe in the dressing area. Leaning over from the seat, I unlocked the safe and pulled out a copy of Tellie's signed confession in which she stated that she had killed her husband, Richard. I compared it to the T on Larry's postcard.

A perfect match!

I laid the postcard, confession, and title transfer of the Prius on the bed. All the T's looked the same. So Tellie was contacting Larry.

Unlocking the bedroom door, I went into my office and pulled out the files I had kept on Richard Pidgeon, Tellie's murdered husband. Looking through my notes, I read where I had written that I thought Larry had lied to me about Tellie. He said he had stopped by her house and left a check from the Beekeepers Association in her mailbox. At Richard's funeral, I saw Larry hand Tellie a piece of paper. When I asked him about it at Lady Elsmere's dinner party, he said it was the check. He also said to mind my own business.

There was another detail nagging at the back of my mind. I went through some more of my notes.

Found it!

When I had confronted Tellie about Richard's death, she said she had lied to her friend Joyce; that she had met someone special and was going to meet him as a cover story for leaving town. Maybe there was truth to the story after all. Maybe she was meeting someone, but then I popped up and confronted her about murdering her husband. Her plans had to be changed after that.

I didn't turn Tellie over to the police because I believed her story that Richard had horribly abused her and she was fearful that he would try to kill her if she tried to leave him. Women get killed in this state all the time while the courts just slap the men's wrists. I thought her story was true and justified.

But maybe I was the sucker in this story.

Maybe she did meet someone special and they decided to kill Richard partly because he was a dangerous nuisance; but also because of the insurance money and the inheritance that Richard's daughter would collect from the death of Richard's first wife, Agnes Bledsoe. That put a different spin on Richard's death.

One way was self-defense was how I looked at it. Another way was pre-meditated murder for profit – first degree.

Larry and Tellie? Could that be possible?

I dialed my cell phone. "Hi, Goetz. Got a minute? I need to know something. Was O'nan assigned to Richard Pidgeon's case or did he request it? Huh? No, I won't leave it alone. Just tell me, okay? . . . Thanks, Goetz." I hung up the phone.

I cradled my head in my hands. I was such an idiot. Couldn't believe how stupid I had been. Hadn't the honeybees taught me how everything is connected – earth, plants, bees, food, and humans? Nothing is coincidental. I should have connected the dots.

I reached for the phone but stopped myself. I couldn't call Matt. I had already driven a wedge between him and Franklin because of my neediness. I couldn't call Asa. I had disrupted her life for almost a year. She had done enough.

Oh, where was Jake? I really needed him.

I sniffled. It didn't take long for the waterworks to turn on full blast. I boohooed until I came up with a new angle. Dialing the phone, I held my breath until it was picked up.

"Hello?"

"Help me, Obi-Wan Kenobi. You're my only hope."

14

Franklin snorted, "What do you want, Josiah?"

"I need you to drive me to Frankfort right now. I am worn out and afraid that I'll wreck if I drive any more today."

"Oh, stop teasing me with good possibilities."

"Be that way. I'll just call Matt and have him help me."

"NOOOO! I'll be over in a few minutes."

"Good," I sneered before hanging up.

Then I dialed Clay. "Hey, Clay. Do you have any more pictures of your softball team or any other team of that era? . . . You do? That's great. Will you be there at work an hour from now? . . . Good. Will you put together all the softball pictures you have? Thanks. See you in a few."

Going into the kitchen, I spied a note from the Todd family saying they had gone to see a movie. I left a note telling them to make sure all the windows and doors were still locked when they got home. Following my own advice, I checked them while waiting for Franklin. It wasn't long before I heard his car's motor. I ran outside to meet him.

"Just drive," I ordered, getting in.

"Where to?"

"Frankfort – to the bee store."

"Why?"

"I think Larry Bingham knew O'nan years ago and got him to request the Pidgeon case."

"Why would he care?"

"Because he was having an affair with Tellie Pidgeon and they planned Richard's death for the insurance money."

Franklin lost control of the car and almost swerved off the road into a slave wall. "Are you out of your mind?" he yelled at me once he got the car under control.

I quickly told him about Larry lying to me about a note he gave Tellie at Richard's funeral and that I found postcards from her on his desk.

"You're reaching," cautioned Franklin. "No hard proof."

"I can have the handwriting analyzed. I know it will match."

"So Tellie writes to him. She might write to a dozen people in Lexington that you know nothing about. She's never been charged with anything."

"Then why all the subterfuge?"

"Because of Daffy Taffy, her daughter?"

"I talked the DA into dropping those charges. See, it all adds up – the private post office box, the lies about the check. He was passing something to Tellie at the funeral and lied about it. I bet it was a note to leave town. He knew I was getting close to finding out that she killed Richard."

"People lie all the time. I lie. You lie."

"Goetz told me that O'nan requested the Pidgeon case."

"So what?"

"Come on, Franklin. Use a little imagination."

"He heard the body was on your farm and used it as an excuse to give you grief."

"Maybe he was given a little nudge to take the case. I just can't believe that after all those years, O'nan still hated my guts for getting him kicked off the UK baseball team."

"I would hate you still."

"I don't care what you say. The answer is in Frankfort. I'll find the connection there."

"Whatever you say," he grumbled, shifting gears.

"Once you eliminate the impossible, whatever remains, however improbable, must be the truth."

"Aristotle?"

"Sherlock Holmes."

15

Clay stood outside waiting for us with his jacket collar pulled up around his neck, as it had started misting. We hurried inside. Even though the day was warm, the rain caused me to shiver a little.

Or was it the rain?

He guided me over to a large table, which was covered in photographs and handed me a magnifying glass. "I went home to get the rest of them," Clay stated.

"Thanks, Clay. I appreciate it."

When I wasn't more forthcoming, Clay reluctantly declared, "I'll be in my office catching up on my paperwork. Call me when you're finished." Clay gave a questioning look at Franklin.

The gaze may have been due to the fact that Franklin was wearing orange shorts with a dress shirt and purple bow tie. To top off the outfit, his feet were encased in hi-top Converse tennis shoes with small plastic GI Joes tied in the shoestrings.

I just didn't ask anymore about Franklin's outfits.

"I'm her Watson," quipped Franklin, catching Clay's eyes.

"Huh?"

"I'm her Watson."

"Whatever you say, friend."

I sat down and started systematically going through each picture, each face.

"What exactly are we looking for?" asked Franklin.

"Try to find a picture with O'nan in it."

"What?"

"Just imagine him ten or fifteen years younger."

"This is a ridiculous waste of time."

"Franklin, do you want that dinner party with Lady Elsmere or not?"

Franklin plopped down on a bench without further argument and began peering closely at pictures.

After forty-five minutes of searching, we came up blank. I carefully put the photographs back in their box. I went in search of Clay, who was now in the warehouse, taking inventory.

"Did you find what you were looking for?" asked Clay.

"No, I'm sorry to say. I thought surely there was a connection."

"A connection for what?"

"Oh, for some stupid theory I had about Richard Pidgeon's demise." I shook Clay's hand. "Well, thanks, man. I'm sorry for the inconvenience. See ya later."

As I was walking out the entrance, Clay called out, "Did you check the two pictures in the men's bathroom?"

I swirled around and sprinted to the men's room, letting my cane fall on the ground. As Franklin was coming out of the men's room, I pushed past him only to find the walls empty.

"Looking for these?" asked Franklin, grinning. He pointed to two 11x14 photographs taken at the Bluegrass States Game placed on a table. Picking up the magnifying glass I meticulously went through each face. I circled every face that was questionable with a black marker on the glass. Finding Clay and Larry Bingham easily, I decided that O'nan was not in the first picture.

Deflated, I threw the magnifying glass on the table and plopped into a chair. A gray cat jumped on my lap.

"Eureka!" cried Franklin. He put the framed photograph in front of my face and pointed, "There's your friend Clay and four people to the left of him is Larry Bingham. Now look at the third row. Who does that look like to you?"

I smiled. "It looks like a very young O'nan to me."

"You have your proof, Josiah. Larry Bingham and O'nan knew each other and not just in an official capacity. They played in the same Bluegrass Stakes game."

Clay strolled in looking at us curiously.

"Clay, can you identify that man?" I asked pointing to O'nan.

"Sure. That's Fred O'nan. He played softball on my team for a season before switching to another team. I never brought it up considering the bad feelings between the two of you."

I pointed to Larry. "Did Larry know O'nan well?"

"Sure. The whole team went out for beer after each game. I would say that they knew each other. If memory serves me well, Larry gave O'nan a letter of recommendation to join the police force."

Franklin gasped. "Talk about still waters."

"Would you swear to that in a court of law?"

"I could swear that they knew each other but not about the letter. I never saw it. I just remember Larry told me, but that was a long time ago."

"Good enough for me." I gave Clay a big hug. "Can I take this photograph? I want to make copies."

"Sure. What's going on, Josiah?"

"I just solved Richard Pidgeon's murder . . . again."

Clay scratched his head. "I thought it was ruled accidental death. What do you know that I don't? Come on, give."

"Can't right now, Clay. I could still be wrong. But if Larry drops in, will you not say anything? It is really important that you don't say that I was here looking at pictures."

"I hate this cloak and dagger stuff."

I gave him my best-wounded hound dog look. "Please?"

"Okay, but you've got to spill everything once it's over."

I shook his hand. "Deal."

Franklin wrapped up the frame and laid it down carefully in the back of his car. I waved goodbye to Clay, who was locking up.

Once down the road, I said to Franklin, "Let's take the back roads to home. I don't want to drive past Larry's house."

Franklin nodded.

"And Franklin?"

"Yeah."

"You are to scan the photograph and make copies. I want the faces blown up. Don't tell anyone that you have the photograph in your possession – not even Matt. Once you've done that, send the JPEG's to Shaneika office. She will give you a statement for Clay to sign when you return the photograph to him. Clay must sign her statement. I must prove that it was in his possession originally."

"Got it. Will do. Now what's in it for me?"

"Franklin, I am going to give you the biggest coming-out party this town has ever seen . . . no pun intended."

I swear the hair on Franklin's arms rose in girlie anticipation. He grinned and cooed, "Now, you're talking, sister."

16

Mike Connor looked through the large plate glass window of his office located on the upper arena floor. From his bird's eye view, he saw that Mrs. Lambert was putting her show horse through its paces, and in another area, Comanche was being exercised while carefully observed by Ms. Todd and her vet.

Upon seeing Shaneika, Mike whistled. He believed she was the real deal. As for so many others in the horse business, money was not the object of her affections. Ms. Todd lusted after glory – of doing something great.

And he didn't think Shaneika had a chance in hell of achieving it.

For one thing, Mike didn't think Comanche had it in him to win. The horse had to want the glory too and Comanche was just too lazy. Second – Ms. Todd didn't have the resources to invest in Comanche. It took lots of money to make a horse a winner. There were jockeys, trainers, vets, food bills, equipment for the horse and that was just the tip of the iceberg. There were entry fees, travel fees . . . the list went on and on.

Mike watched as the vet and Shaneika engaged in a heated discussion. Wanting to know what they were saying, Mike went to a wall panel and turned on some intercom switches that Lady Elsmere had installed years ago. His employer was not averse to eavesdropping on those who used her training facilities to pick up a tidbit of useful information.

He listened carefully as Shaneika insisted that there was something wrong with Comanche, but the vet kept saying that the horse was sound as a bell. She exhaled in frustration as she watched the vet retreat to his car.

Sitting on a bleacher behind Ms. Todd was Josiah Reynolds who beckoned to her friend to sit down beside her. They talked briefly about the horse and then switched gears.

Mrs. Reynolds began weaving some sort of tale about predators in the early sixties and that she believed that a friend of hers was the real murderer of the guy who was found on her place last year. She sounded like a conspiracy nut.

He would have lots to report to his boss, Lady Elsmere, but first he had to help Ms. Todd, whom he liked a lot.

*

Seeing Mike emerge from his office, I stopped talking and waved as he ambled over to us.

"Ms. Todd, something wrong with your horse?"

"No, nothing. Just having him checked out."

Mike shrugged his powerful shoulders and looked away as though trying to think of what to say next. "This may sound like voodoo, but whenever I have a hunch that something is wrong with one of my horses and the vet can't find nothing – I call this woman." He handed Shaneika a piece of paper with a phone number on it.

"What this?" demanded Shaneika, looking at the number.

"She's fey and very good. She uses a dowsing rod. Now don't laugh. She's never been wrong about what's ailing a horse. She only tells you what's wrong with the animal. She doesn't treat it." He pointed to the paper. "You'll call that woman if you value Comanche."

I couldn't help but smile. Very few people talked to Shaneika with such force. They were too intimidated. Mike was six feet two with massive shoulders and arms. He was a powerfully built man; though he was courteous enough, I knew not to mess with him. We had tangled about some of my animals roaming onto June's property. Mike didn't like that and let me know about it. He believed that strong fences made good neighbors.

I knew lots about Mike. He could trace his ancestry back to those who had been imported decades before the Civil War to build the dry-laid rock walls that encircled the farms in the Bluegrass. I also knew that one of his ancestors was Stephen Foster, who composed *My Old Kentucky Home*, our state song.

Originally Scotch-Irish immigrated to Kentucky in the late 1700s through the Cumberland Gap while the Dutch and Germans migrated down the Ohio River and settled in Northern Kentucky. More Irish came in 1848 due to the potato famine. Many stayed in the area and built some of our little stone churches and taught the slaves to make the stone fences, which is how they got their name of "slave walls." Then Mike's family name had been O'Connor, but through the years they had shortened it to Connor. Today there are over 700,000 descendants of Irish ancestry living in Kentucky. All this I knew about Mike, but I didn't know about the bomb he was going to drop on me next.

"Mrs. Reynolds, I hear that you are helping with the investigation of Mr. Greene's demise. Might I come to your house this afternoon? I'll be off work then and . . . will feel more comfortable talking away from here."

I looked inquisitively at Mike. "Michael, were you spying on us with June's intercom system?"

Mike gave me a lopsided grin. "I accidentally flipped the switch with my elbow, but I didn't hear anything. Honest."

"Talk about blarney," I laughed. "Come over when you're done. We'll both be there."

Mike grinned and went to check on horses in the south pastures.

I tuned to Shaneika. "I think he might be sweet on you."

"He's white," commented Shaneika.

"I've never asked about your ancestry but it looks like you have quite a bit of white blood in you, Shaneika. And then there are the family heirlooms like letters from Abraham Lincoln and vintage couture clothes – not to mention the family name of Todd. Plus your office happens to be in a building with Masonic symbols everywhere. I looked up the history of that building and branches of the Todd family built it and have owned it ever since."

"What are you trying to imply?"

"That you are an interesting woman, Shaneika. And one of these days, I'm going to find out your story," I mused. "If you were to have a family reunion, just who would show up?"

Shaneika's hazel eyes gleamed. "You would be very surprised by who would show up." She laughed heartily. "Very surprised. I'll give you just a taste. I'm related to Dolley Madison."

Knowing that's all she would tell me, I changed the subject. "Mike Connor is a very nice man. You could do worse."

"I don't need any man, white or black, distracting me from Comanche." With that proclamation she strode out of the enclosed arena.

I thought of Jake and how I missed him. I lay awake at nights wishing he were here to help me though this mess I had gotten myself into again. I hoped Shaneika wasn't going to throw away a chance for happiness.

A good man could be a woman's blessing.

If he was no good, he could destroy her by taking her down a rabbit's hole.

17

In Lexington, one can plainly see the past sexual play between whites and blacks even though "intermingling" of the races was illegal well into the twentieth century. A person's skin color is still somewhat used to place a person into a caste system for social and economic control even though lack of an education is more of a barrier now.

In the nineteenth century any child born from a white man and a slave woman automatically inherited the status of the mother and became the property of the father, who could sell the child at whim.

One scandalous case involved the "Tippecanoe and Tyler Too" President John Tyler who, in 1841, brought to Washington one James Hambleton Christian, his wife's slave, but also his wife's half-brother. Tyler, even fathered a slave son himself, John Dunjee, a prominent educator and minister.

But people are people no matter what station in life and sometimes these relationships were built on love and devotion. Take the case of Richard M. Johnson, ninth vice president of the U.S., who had a lengthy relationship with a Julia Chinn, who bore him two daughters. These daughters were acknowledged by Johnson and given the same rank and privileges white daughters could expect from a wealthy father even though the law considered them black and slaves. He even arranged advantageous marriages with white men and gave the girls large dowries. In his will, he deeded them his property, which shocked Bluegrass society.

More often, though, white men used black women as a sexual outlet, as in the case of Mary Todd Lincoln's cousin, John Todd Russell, whose only son was born from a slave. After John's death, his mother freed the grandson and mother.   Was this Shaneika's namesake?

I shook my head. No, Shaneika's last name was Todd, not Russell. There had to be a closer connection.

I was mulling this over while watching Mike enter through the bamboo alcove on my console screen. I met him at the front door and welcomed him in.

I poured him a bourbon on the rocks while explaining that Shaneika was taking a shower.

Mrs. Todd was in the pool with Lincoln.

Of course, Baby sat next to the pool – his eyes glued on the boy splashing in the water. I was beginning to wonder about Baby's obsession with Lincoln. Was Baby guarding him? Did he dream of eating Lincoln if given the chance or did he think Lincoln was another dog?

"That's okay," replied Mike when told that Shaneika would be a few more minutes. "I really wanted to speak with you. I hope you don't think I'm a gossip monger."

"You know something, Mike?"

"Just what I heard myself."

"With your little intercom system?"

"Maybe. I don't want to give the impression that I turn that thing on all the time. It is actually used to communicate with workers on the arena floor. It just so happens that I had been talking with my floor guys and forgot to turn it off." He hesitated for a moment.

"Arthur Greene was with Aspen Lancaster in the arena shortly before Arthur died and things got pretty heated."

"Well, tell me what they said," I requested as I began talking notes.

"Aspen was fed up with what he referred to as the crumbs from the dinner table. He told Arthur that he wanted a percentage of Arthur's horse, Dancing Ruby, and nothing else would do. Then Aspen said something funny."

"What was it?"

"'Lots of guys are still pissed on how they were snookered. Maybe I should tell them what really went down.'"

"What happened then?" I asked.

"Arthur turned white as a sheet and cursed at Aspen, who just laughed."

"Did Aspen threaten to kill or harm Arthur?"

"No."

"What do you think Aspen was referring to?"

"I haven't the slightest idea."

"Would you make an official statement about what you told me?"

"Not at this time. Aspen is still out there and is very powerful in the horse racing business. I don't want to make an enemy of him, but if the shoe drops and other evidence comes out that he had something to do with Arthur Greene's death, then I'll make a statement. Until then, this is just gossip."

"I understand," I replied.

I really did.

18

Several weeks later, Matt and I were guests of Lady Elsmere's at a horse awards dinner, where all the top players in the horse business got together and played. They slapped each other's backs and gave out awards while drinking copious amounts of champagne and other liver-damaging liquids. Because of June's pull, Shaneika was invited, though hers was the only dark face at the tables besides the Middle Eastern players.

I was scanning the banquet room for faces I knew when my tired eyes rested on Agnes Bledsoe.

Jumping Jehosaphat, wasn't she dead yet!

While I was talking to the other guests at the table, I kept one eye on her. I had to admit, though in her middle sixties, Agnes was still a stunning woman, and like bees to honey, men flitted around her. Other than smiling she gave them no encouragement and did not ask anyone to sit down to the empty seat beside her.

After poking at my dried-out chicken patty covered with some kind of slimy gravy and listening to several inebriated speeches, I excused myself, following Agnes into the foyer and then to the lobby's bar.

She sat at the bar and ordered two drinks. Turning, she beckoned.

I clumsily climbed on the stool next to her. "I see the cancer hasn't gotten you yet, Agnes."

She gave me the once over. "I heard about your fall. I must say you look like shit."

"You should have seen me before they cleaned me up." I pointed at her head. "See you still wearing that wig, Agnes. Bald as a cantaloupe?"

A shadow of a smile crossed her lips. "Defiant to the end, eh, Josiah. I like that. I propose a toast to the two meanest bitches in Lexington."

"Sometimes being a bitch is all a woman has to hold onto," I quoted from *Dolores Claiborne*.

"And the critics say Stephen King can't write," Agnes sarcastically purred. "Now, what do you want?"

"You know anything about hard feelings between Aspen Lancaster and Arthur Greene?"

"Ask me something difficult." She took a sip of her drink. "Now what's in it for me if I tell you what you want to know."

"I'll tell you something about Richard's wife, Tellie. Tit for tat."

"Darling. It will have to be your tit for tat as my tits are gone. Cancer got them." She pulled a cigarette out of her purse and asked the bartender for a light. "Okay, I'll bite. You tell me first what you know about the missing Miss Tellie and I will tell you what I know."

I told her about the postcard I found at Larry Bingham's honey house and how it had that distinctive T that Tellie made. I also told her about his lies to me about something he slipped her at Richard's funeral. I told her everything except that Tellie had confessed that she killed Richard. Finally I ran out of steam and sat nursing my drink.

Agnes finished hers and motioned to the bartender for another. "I want a copy of the post card. Can you make me one?"

I nodded.

"I will send a courier to your house tomorrow. Have it ready," she ordered.

"Is Taffy still your heir?"

"Of course, she's Richard's daughter. I have no one else. You don't think she had anything to do with her father's death?"

"I am pretty sure she didn't."

"But you think Tellie might have?"

"Now I've given you something. Your turn."

"You know that Aspen and Arthur were best friends in college and on the football team together. Well, Arthur quit the team right before the '62 fall season but Aspen stayed on."

"Why?"

"He was a poor boy from the mountains who was on a scholarship. If he quit the team, he lost the scholarship.

"The football coaches were hounding players who quit to sign away their scholarship rights. Aspen had no other option for college other than stick it out on that football team or else rob a bank to pay for school."

"And Arthur?"

"Arthur had other options, so he took a powder. They were still tight for years after that, but things soured between them in the late eighties. Arthur was a business genius and soared ahead while Aspen plugged along. Aspen became bitter that Arthur didn't carry him."

"Why didn't he?"

"How far should a friend go to make sure that his best friend has the same amount of money in the bank? That kind of responsibility can be exhausting and it's not fair to either person. Aspen should have let go of Arthur but wouldn't. Still – when Aspen lost his horse farm to bankruptcy, Arthur hired him as a trainer and encouraged his friends to do the same."

"How is Aspen as a trainer?"

"You would want to give him your second string of horses to play with – not your grand champions."

"In other words, adequate but not great."

Agnes nodded her head. "The last five years, Aspen has been working as a breeder for several horse farms. He takes care of the paperwork but wants back out on the track. Training is much more glamorous than breeding."

"What about Dancing Ruby?"

"Arthur thought he might be a Triple Crown contender. Aspen wanted to train him. Arthur said no, but Aspen kept begging, threatening."

"The police say that Aspen has an airtight alibi."

"Alibis can be bought."

"You think he did it?"

"I don't think. I only give out what I know for sure. I verify my information."

"Anything else?"

"Aspen is known for being vindictive, which is probably why Arthur wanted to keep him at arm's length at times. Arthur was good to Aspen, and Aspen, even with all his meanness, loved Arthur like a brother for the most part. That never stopped."

"The bone yard is filled with people murdered by those who loved them."

Agnes signed. "I'm tired, Josiah. I don't want to talk about this anymore."

I swiveled off my chair and picked up my cane. "Thanks for the drink."

"Let's not make a habit of this," Agnes quipped, smiling bitterly.

I limped back into the banquet room, knowing that Agnes' dark eyes were blazing into my back.

It takes a lot of courage to turn your back on that woman.

19

An owl hooting at the morning sun rising over the eastern ridge woke me up. I groggily climbed out of bed and let the rambunctious kittens out to meet their mother, who had taken to nighttime hunting. She would surely have a treat for them. It was okay as long as none of my songbirds were part of the cache.

My left leg was throbbing. I reached under my nightgown and pulled off my pain patch while calling for Jake on the baby intercom.

He didn't come.

Irritated, I stumbled into his bedroom and turned on the light switch. His bed was neatly made and the dresser was cleared of his possessions. Rubbing the sleep from my eyes, I remembered that he was gone.

Plopping down on the side of the bed, I reached for the pillow and deeply inhaled. It still retained remnants of Jake's smell. I realized why I hadn't washed the sheets yet. This was the last physical contact I had of him.

"Excuse me," said Mrs. Todd, poking in her head.

"That's all right. Come on in."

Mrs. Todd, in her night robe, entered the room and sat in a corner chair. "I didn't mean to intrude, but I heard you get up. Just wanted to check on you." She pulled her robe tightly while crossing her legs. "You know honey, this is none of my business, but you can't live in this house alone. At least not for the time being."

I nodded miserably. "I've got seven more months of therapy left. I guess the worst thing is that I'm afraid of falling and not being able to crawl to a phone."

Mrs. Todd smiled. "I have the same fear. I've got a bad hip, but my baby calls me twice a day." She leaned forward, whispering. "I have a secret dream that we'll buy a house together. I could be a big help with Lincoln but Shaneika values her privacy, so I guess that won't happen." She gave a deep, rich chuckle. "I remember not wanting my mother around too."

I looked away not really wanting to face that we were two lonely women. I didn't want to hear it. I didn't want to accept it. My bottom lip started to quiver.

She continued. "Now I'm too old to find another man, but you have time still." She cocked her head. "Shaneika told me about this Jake fellow and how he quickly disappeared. She said you've acted funny ever since."

I bitterly laughed. "I loved my husband very much and for most of our marriage we were in synch. You know what I mean?"

Mrs. Todd nodded.

"We liked the same movies, same food, voted for the same political party, and had similar goals. We were married for twenty-eight years and twenty of those years were fabulous. You couldn't have asked for a better partner. Maybe there were problems and I just looked the other way. I don't really know except that I was happy for the most part.

"Now Jake and I have nothing in common. We can't even agree on what TV show to watch, but I ache for Jake the way I never ached for my husband. All I seem to think about is the heat of his skin when touching mine, how the back of my neck tingled when I caught him looking at me. This neediness for him runs so deep inside me that sometimes I think I won't able to take the next breath. He kissed me one time and I thought I was going to faint." I shook my head. "A simple kiss. I can't explain it except that I felt I had dropped into a black void where there was only sensation. I simply lost myself in him."

"You got love sickness the worst I've seen for a long time," replied Mrs. Todd. "Why don't you call him?"

I shook my head in despair. "Asa sent him away. Unless things are made right between the two of them, I have to give him up. She is my blood, bone of my bone, my flesh. I can't go against my daughter."

"Like the biblical Ruth and her mother-in-law."

"Something like that."

We both heard Lincoln roll out of bed chattering to Baby, who had taken to sleeping with him. Mrs. Todd gave me a sympathetic look while helping me rise off the bed. She went to Lincoln's room while I stumbled around looking for where I had placed the box of pain patches.

I felt dull and listless. The only thing alive about me was the pain.

And I hated it.

20

In the thirties, Jean Harlow was one of the biggest stars at MGM, or in the world for that matter. Studio executives discovered her as she waited for a friend in a car. Harlow claimed that her platinum hair was real. It was that white hair that made her the screen's first sex goddess – more so than Greta Garbo, Gloria Swanson or Mae West. Her film *Red-Headed Woman* created a furor over its plot in which a woman sleeps her way to success and suffers no retribution for it. She got clean away, enjoying the high life. The moral backlash was one more reason to force the studio heads to allow the Hays Commission to censor their films.

But instead of a boycott, Harlow's next film made even more money. Go figure.

In the end it didn't matter. She died at the age of 26 from renal failure. Her great love, William Powell, the

elegant actor of *The Thin Man* series, left a note in her
dead hand – *Goodnight, my dearest darling.*

The Jean Harlow that stood before me at the
September yearling sales at Keeneland Race Track was
not a blond but a gleaming brunette with four white
stocking legs. She was brought in by a Hispanic worker,
who handed her over to an African-American handler
wearing a green Keeneland sports coat. The white
auctioneers presided like high priests over the event.

I sat in the back of the pavilion filled with
international and local buyers with money to burn. They
had one thing in common – they loved horses and the
kingly sport of Thoroughbred racing. It was their
passion. Their raison d'être.

The Keeneland sales have had many "interesting"
spectators over the years. One was a Mrs. Emile
Denemark, who was rumored to be Al Capone's sister.
She was remembered wearing an apricot lace dress with a
Chihuahua thrust into her ample bosom. Whenever Mrs.
Denemark took a deep breath, the Chihuahua's eyes
would bulge out of his head and then recede when she
exhaled.

The reason I was at Keeneland was to watch Aspen
Lancaster sell his own horse, Jean Harlow. The sire had
been Arthur's Dancing Ruby, which was unusual in itself.
Horses still in their racing career are rarely used as stud
horses, but apparently a special deal had been worked out
between Arthur and Aspen – at least that's what Aspen
said.

And he did have the video, semen sample, and paperwork to prove it.

Aspen sat in the third row, his face blank. How did it feel to sell a possible Kentucky Derby winner – Aspen's last chance at immortality? His face simply didn't register. But everyone knew Aspen needed money – his creditors would swallow whatever the horse brought.

The bidding started. I trained my binoculars on Aspen's face. I heard the auctioneer start at $10,000.

Bidder from Dubai raised a finger.

"Do I hear 20,000, 20, 20, bid it up, 20, 20?"

An Asian man nodded very discreetly. A spotter yelled what sounded like, "Yep!"

"Thank you. Now do I hear 30,000, 30, 30, 30? Bid it up here. Hear 30, 30, 30? Bid it up here."

Spotters, standing on the floor, surveyed the room.

The bidding continued with four bidders until the amount reached $1 million. People started rushing into the sales pavilion from outside. There was a hush inside the room. I saw Aspen's hand twitch.

"Bid it up here. Do I hear 1,250,000, 250, 250, 250, 250?"

Once again the bidder from Dubai raised his index finger. The spotter pointed.

The room's excitement escalated.

"Thank you. Do I hear 1,350,000, bid it up here, 350, 350, 350? Bid it up here."

The bidder for a sheikh nodded. People were now standing on chairs surveying the room. The bidding advanced as the man from Ireland rubbed his nose.

The sheikh and the Irishman went bid for bid until the sum reached two million.

"Thank you. Do I hear 2,100,000, 100, 100? Bid it up here."

Spotters simultaneously raised their hands and yelled, "Yep!!!" Their color was flushed with excitement.

Up and up the sum crawled until it reached $3 million. A spotter pointed and yelled.

"Thank you. Now do I hear 3,100,000, 100, 100?"

I swiveled my head to see who had just bid. There sat Lady Elsmere sat with a smug expression on her face. Beside her was Charles, who nodded.

A gasp arose from the crowed.

"Thank you. Now do I hear 3,200,000, 200, 200?"

The buyer for the sheikh looked at his boss for approval and nodded.

"Thank you. Now do I hear 3,300,000, 300, 300?"

The Irish buyer raised his hand, giving the sheikh a nasty look.

"Thank you. Bid it up here. Do I hear 3,400,000, 400, 400?"

The sheikh shook his head, but a spotter yelled, "Yep."

We all stretched our necks to see who else had bid. The Irish buyer looked smug.

"Do I hear 3,500,000, 500, 500, 500?"

Charles nodded.

"Thank you. Do I hear 3,600,000, 600, 600, 600? Last bid. No?"

The Irish buyer swirled his head to glare at Lady Elsmere who returned a sweet smile.

Everyone stared from under their programs at the Irish buyer including Aspen. Some people, like myself, craned their necks to get a better look. The Irishman slumped back in his chair while shaking his head.

"HIP 56 goes for $3,500,000. Congratulations to the buyer." The auctioneer banged his gavel.

Lady Elsmere stood and waved to a cheering crowd.

People were slapping Aspen's back. In response he shook off their enthusiasm and strode off after giving his filly one last look.

After the crowd around Lady Elsmere dissipated, I made my way towards her and Charles.

I spoke just one word. "Why?"

June looked like a cat that had just licked up all the cream in the pitcher. "Arthur was beholden to Aspen. I knew he would want me to take care of him. This is Aspen's last chance for a Derby winner and mine as well."

"What about My Lady Elizabeth's foal?"

"Maybe I'll have two Derby winners before I die. Anyway time is running out for me. I'm taking a shortcut in case Liz's foal doesn't take."

"Who is going to train Jean Harlow? Only a few fillies have ever won the Kentucky Derby."

June's eyes shone with excitement. "Look at her, Josiah. Look at her chest. Her thighs. She's a born winner. She's got the fire in her eyes to win."

I glanced at Charles.

"She knows horses, Miss Josiah. If Lady Elsmere says this horse is a winner, then she's a winner. She's rarely wrong."

"Let's not talk about the fact that you paid three million too much for that horse and you have set a record for horseflesh – you didn't answer my question, who is going to train Jean Harlow?"

"Aspen, of course."

"Aspen?"

"Yes, why not."

"Because he might have been the one who killed Arthur."

"Tosh, he has an airtight alibi which no one has been able to break. He was at the party next door until he went home. He's got dozens of witnesses."

"But that party took place right next door to the Royal Blue Stables. Doesn't that seem odd to you?"

"Aspen didn't do it," June countered emphatically. "He didn't do it. He's an old man. He would not have had the strength to hoist Arthur up to the rafters. He's got terrible arthritis. He couldn't physically have committed that murder."

"Why do you say that? Do you know who did? Why was Arthur beholden to Aspen?"

"Josiah, don't spoil my glorious day. I've got an offspring from Arthur's Dancing Ruby and his best friend is going to train Jean Harlow to win the Derby for me. It is the last thing I can do for my darling Arthur."

Some well wishers came over. June turned and joyfully greeted them. I knew I had been dismissed. That was okay. I needed to think. June was right on one thing. Aspen was too weak to have killed Arthur by strangulation and then have hoisted him to the rafters unless he had had help. Perhaps I should be looking for a younger, stronger man.

21

Comanche was safely ensconced in a stall along with Shaneika, the vet, and myself waiting for Mike Connor's witchy-woman, Velvet Maddox. Finally we saw dust stirring on the gravel road and soon a beat-up farm truck emerged from a brown cloud to abruptly stop in front of the barn. A spry little elf of a woman, who was no bigger than a worn-out piece of soap, hopped out of the dusty cab carrying a carpetbag. She strode up to the vet. "Let's get this show on the road. I've got beans to pick."

The vet, startled by this introduction, opened his mouth but no sound came out. He just looked confused.

Shaneika had the presence of mind to say, "This way, please. Comanche is rather feisty today."

"He won't be," assured the little elf. "Animals take to me."

I followed, sharply observing Velvet Maddox decked out in polyester pants and. cheap blouse purchased from a discount store. On her hand, though, was a fabulous emerald ring. Also her white hair was smartly done and her toenails, sticking out from her expensive sandals, were professionally painted. Hmmm, no boots. No boots around a horse? Not a good thing.

Velvet Maddox thought certain items about her life warranted getting the best. Clothes did not fall into that category.

Shaneika opened Comanche's stall. The black brute came towards his owner, nudging her shoulder for peppermints. Shaneika's face softened as she gave him some and rubbed his neck.

"Can you walk him up and down for me?" requested Miss Velvet. She watched intently as the horse moved before her.

"I can't find anything wrong with this horse," whined the vet. "It is beyond me why he won't do his best. He just doesn't have it in him."

Shaneika shot the vet a dark look. "Shush, he can hear you."

Miss Velvet sighed. Reaching into her carpetbag, she pulled out two dowsing rods that looked like they had been cut from wire coat hangers. She quickly said a prayer and asked the rods to look for sickness in the horse.

Comanche neighed, looking suspiciously at rods.

"Now hold him tight," commanded Miss Velvet. She pointed her dowsing rods at the horse in her tiny hands with firm conviction. Starting at the back end, she moved slowly around Comanche's legs, then his sides, and his middle, underneath his belly. Nothing. The dowsing rods did not move.

The vet smirked.

Then she moved towards his head on the right side. Nothing.

Shaneika looked downcast as she moved under the horse's neck so Miss Velvet could move on the left side.

With tightened lips, Miss Velvet moved on the left side of the horse's face. Suddenly the dowsing rods converged at Comanche's left eye. "Hmmmm," was all Miss Velvet commented as she moved down the left side again. The rods immediately uncrossed, standing straight out before her. Miss Velvet went around the horse again until she came to the left side of Comanche's face. Again, the rods converged at the horse's left eye.

Clucking, Miss Velvet wiped off her dowsing rods before placing them back in her carpetbag satchel.

Shaneika put Comanche back into his stall.

Waving a crooked, wrinkled finger at the vet, Miss Velvet beckoned him to her. Towering over her, he stood like a little boy about to be whipped for stealing his mother's cigarettes . . . or maybe her lipstick.

Shaneika stood beside him, looking expectantly.

"That horse has got pus around the left eye. Get rid of the pus and he will do what you want him to."

"There is no sign of any eye infection," retorted the vet.

"I didn't say the eye was infected. I said pus was around the eye. Now don't use any antibiotics. Just give him warm water and salt. Go up through the nose several times. That ought to break the pus ball. Let him snort it out. Make sure he drains real good. If that ball won't break, then you're going to have to punch it." She picked up her bag and made way for the car. "Good day" was all she said before she drove away.

Shaneika looked at me.

I shrugged my shoulders. "It couldn't hurt," I suggested. "Warm water and salt." All the time I was wondering if Miss Velvet used her rods on people. I could use some help in that area myself.

"It's stupid," admonished the vet.

"Let's do it. We've got nothing to lose," replied Shaneika.

The vet got out some saline solution and warmed it on his SUV's hood five minutes. Then he inserted a tube up Comanche's nose and forced the saline solution into the nose cavity. This is not an easy task – if you want to stay alive. Each time Comanche got meaner.

Third time's a charm. Something broke. Comanche waved his head widely and yellow water drained out of his nostril.

After another two hours and two more treatments, both horse and humans were exhausted but Comanche's nose drippings were running clear. The vet left looking like a chastised dog caught chomping the family's dinner pork roast. Shaneika bedded down in the barn to keep an eye on her beloved stallion, which was munching contently from his bucket of oats.

I drove home in my golf cart. As was my habit, I checked the security system monitors after I let myself in. The cop car was still at the entrance of the driveway, but I knew it was a matter of time before it was pulled off duty.

Mrs. Todd was snoring in an easy chair with the local newspaper collapsing in disarray from her lap to the floor. Lincoln was also on the floor in his room cuddling with Baby, who opened his good eye when I peeked into the room. I quietly put a blanket on both of them. Baby yawned and went back to sleep. I thought everyone had the right idea. So I went to sleep too after I checked all the doors and windows . . . not that I was paranoid.

22

I awoke to a tapping sound. Sitting up, I rubbed my eyes and gave my room a confused look around.

My eyes rested on the patio door where Larry Bingham was standing. He had a weird smile on his face, one that I had never seen before.

I gasped.

He mouthed for me to open the door.

I groggily shook my head while stumbling into the bathroom until I splashed my face with cold water, shaking out the cobwebs.

Had I been dreaming? Just in case I got out a stun gun from a shoebox. Then I heard a padding of paws and a low growl. I limped back into my bedroom.

I hadn't been dreaming.

Larry was standing at my patio glass door looking very amused at Baby who was warning him not to try the door.

"Let me in," mouthed Larry.

I shook my head again, pointing to my cell phone. I held the stun gun right at him. I knew if he had a gun, the bullet could not penetrate the thick glass especially installed.

Larry got out his phone and dialed.

I answered at the first ring.

Larry gave me that creepy smile again. "Josiah, do you have a postcard that belongs to me?"

"I don't know what you are talking about," I answered, never taking my eyes off him.

Neither did Baby.

"I think you do, toots. After you came to see me the other day, I found the top of my desk different from what I had left it and a postcard from under the desk calendar was missing."

I said nothing.

"And from the suspicious way you are treating an old friend, I can guess you have put some pieces of the puzzle together." He smiled again.

That smile scared the crap out of me. I had to sit on the bed as my legs were shaking. "Are you a friend?" I asked.

"Actually I am," replied Larry, his very blue eyes never blinking. "I just didn't realize how much Fred hated you. That was my mistake. I've felt guilty about it ever since."

"But not about killing Richard Pidgeon."

Larry's eyes blinked. He smiled again but his eyes did not look friendly. "Now, you know that has been declared an accidental death. No proof of foul play whatsoever and his body has been cremated." He switched the phone to his other ear. "Nothing can be tied to me. Forget it, Jake, it's Chinatown."

I continued. "Tellie confessed to me that she killed Richard by injecting adrenaline into his neck and using the bee stings to cover up the marks. I have a signed confession and a recording."

"Yeah, about that. I'm going to have to have those too, Josiah."

I shook my head. "I let her go because she was a battered woman fighting for her life. But she also told me that she gave her friend Joyce a false story that she had met a man. Now I'm thinking that maybe the story was true. She had met someone and it is this someone who planned Richard's death to gain both Tellie and the money that would eventually come to her."

"I always told you that you were smart, Josiah. That sharp brain of yours is going to cut your nose off." He rattled the door angrily.

Baby immediately started barking and reared up on the glass. I pulled him down and away from the window. Baby leaned against me, lowly growling at Larry.

"Why did you sic Fred O'nan on me?"

"Did I?"

"You just said you didn't realize how much O'nan hated me, but he went too far, didn't he? You were just trying to throw the police off your track. You knew O'nan for many years, played on the same softball team together. He must have told you about our past history."

"Fantastical story."

"I think you and Tellie fell in love . . . or she fell in love with you. Maybe you did love her. Anyway you wanted Richard dead so you planned the murder and you carried it out. Not Tellie. She lied for you."

He shook his head.

"You gave her a note at Richard's funeral telling her to leave town . . . that I was getting too close. And you sent Fred to the funeral to scare me off the case. He would have done anything for you. He looked up to you. Was it your idea to have my house ransacked?"

"What is going on in here?"

I turned to see Mrs. Todd in the doorway staring at me.

I turned back to the window.

Larry was gone.

23

It was late by the time Detective Goetz left. He politely listened to my story, carefully took notes, confirmed that Mrs. Todd had seen a man standing at my bedroom patio door before he bolted.

"You know there is nothing I can do about this," said Goetz after Mrs. Todd left for bed. Shaneika and I looked at each other.

"Unless Bingham confesses to killing Richard Pidgeon, nothing can be done as there is no evidence. Just your story . . . which is your second theory of how Richard died," he continued as I started to object. He held up his hand to silence me. "I can go talk to him and suggest that he not come to your bedroom door, but you can't even get him on trespassing as you have given him free range to work your bees at his convenience. All charges were dropped against Taffy Pidgeon as you wished and there are no charges against her mother Tellie. In the end it is

140

just your word against his since you have no hard
evidence and never will. Richard was cremated.

"Now I am going to give you a piece of advice. Quit
sticking your nose in other people's business or it's going
to get punched."

"Gee, let me write that down," I huffed. "People are
sure worried about my nose."

Goetz gave me a hard look before putting his
notebook in his pocket along with his stubby pencil.

"Thank you, Detective, for coming all the way out
here," said Shaneika. "Let me show you out."

"He said to me, 'Forget it, Jake, it's Chinatown.'"

"So?"

"That line is from the movie *Chinatown*. Ever seen it?"

"A long time ago."

"It's about a private investigator who uncovers
corruption and murder in Los Angeles over the water
supply but no one will listen. Chinatown is a place but
also refers to mysteries that will remain clouded forever.
Richard Pidgeon's death will remain clouded forever.
What really happened will never unravel. Larry was
telling me so."

Goetz stood. He had lost weight recently and his
pants were dangerously low on his hips. "Like I said, you
keep sticking your nose around, it's gonna get punched."

"You mean like someone pulling me off an eighty-foot
cliff," I replied.

Goetz ignored me but followed Shaneika saying, "I
know my way."

Before Shaneika came back, I went to check on Lincoln.

Satisfied that danger had past, Baby had returned to Lincoln's side and was taking up most of the bed. In order to compensate, Lincoln was half lying on Baby with the kittens taking up what little space was left. As cramped as they were, each wore a look of total bliss, taking comfort in each other's company.

I fled to my room and shut the door. It was very late or very early depending on how you looked at it. Taking a hot shower, I went over the events of today. Goetz was right. There was nothing I could do and nothing I could prove.

I was in Chinatown.

And I could get into serious trouble. Sooner or later . . . if I kept pursuing this . . . it would come out that I thought Tellie was the murderer and let her go. I would be booked as an accomplice after the fact to murder. It was not in my best interest to pursue the Richard Pidgeon case any longer.

For several hours I tossed and turned. I stared out the window. I listen to myself breathe. I went through old memories. I picked up the phone and then put it back.

I paced back and forth in my room.

I couldn't stand being alone.

Finally I put on my best negligee and robe, combed my hair and put on some makeup. I also put some panties, a shirt, and a pair of pants in a bag. Quietly as I could, I snuck out of the house and, taking the golf cart, made my way to Matt's little house.

Matt opened the door, pushing back black, unruly hair. "What's wrong?"

"I can't sleep. I don't want to be by myself tonight." Spying my bag, Matt gave my negligee-clothed body the once-over. "I don't think this is a good idea, Josiah," he responded in a quiet voice.

"Don't make me beg," I replied. "Franklin never has to know. Please. I can't be alone tonight."

Matt stepped out of the way and made way for his bedroom.

I came inside and silently closed the door.

24

After I finally fell asleep, I had dreams – but not of Matt.

I dreamt that I followed Jake into the horse barn. A storm was brewing and Jake's black Indian hair whipped wildly about his face. Upon hearing me call his name, he turned towards me. His eyes looked expectantly at me as his lips slightly opened. I pushed him against a post and kissed him hard. Then I ripped his white shirt open, kissing and teasing his nipples. He murmured my name and tried to hold me but I bound his hands with horse reins. Jake moaned.

I suddenly awoke.

Matt was already gone.

After taking a shower, I hurriedly dressed and then made every effort to erase my presence from the house. I stripped the bed and washed the sheets, knowing that Franklin was like a bloodhound and would smell me.

144

Washing the bourbon glasses Matt and I had used, I then swept the floor, made sure all my night things were in my bag, made the bed. I even checked under the bed to make sure nothing of mine was there. By 9:30 a.m., I was in my golf cart heading home. If anyone there asked where I had been, my answer was that I had been up early checking on my bees.

Did I feel guilty? Hell no.

Maybe that would come. But not for a while.

I knew Matt slept with some of his women clients if he thought it would help him rise on the corporate ladder. Matt was very ambitious and not above some hanky-panky if it would give him a leg up.

I knew he would not turn me down.

I just didn't want Franklin to find out, as I knew he sensed something was already going on with Matt.

Franklin was a confident gay man. He wouldn't understand Matt's proclivities and confusion about his sexuality.

When I got home, everyone was gone. Shaneika to work, Lincoln to school, and Mrs. Todd checking on her own house. I gave a sigh of relief.

Later that afternoon, I received a large bouquet of yellow roses. The card read: "Thank you for a memorable night. One that I will always cherish. M."

Always the gentleman, Matt was telling me politely our night together was a one-time thing only, but our friendship was intact. The color yellow symbolized friendship.

I threw the flowers over the cliff.

25

Detective Goetz called that afternoon. "Got some interesting news for you. Your boy, Larry, has left town."

"How did you find this out?"

"I went to visit him and his wife returned from out of town about the same time."

"Brenda?"

"Yeah. She said she had been visiting her mother but that Larry was not returning her calls. She called a neighbor to check, but he said no one would answer the door but Larry's car was in the driveway. So she came home in a hurry."

"What did you find?"

"I went into the house expecting to find him dead from a heart attack, but got a little surprise. A suitcase and some of his clothes were gone. The bedroom was a mess. Looked like he had packed in a hurry. Found a note left on the bed saying that Larry was leaving Brenda and for her to get a divorce."

"Brenda called the bank and found that Larry had taken $50,000 out of their joint accounts."

"Did he give a reason why he was leaving?"

"No, except that he was tired of the marriage and wanted to start over."

"Oh, poor Brenda."

"She was pretty devastated."

"Was this a surprise to her or did she suspect something was wrong?"

"Completely new to her. She thought they were fine. She has no idea why he bolted." Goetz shifted his weight. "He left something for you, Josiah."

"Me?"

"Mrs. Bingham gave it to me to give to you." He handed me a sealed box.

I smiled. "I know you have already opened this with steam."

Goetz gave me a cockeyed grin. "What makes you say that?"

"Because it would be what I would do if I were in your shoes." I tore open the small box and found a note.

Dear Josiah,

You play a mean game of chess. You have checked, but in the end I will checkmate because I will be living the life I want to. Don't worry about me, but the knight is one crazy son of a bitch. Watch out for him."

In it was a chess knight carved out of beeswax.

"What do you think?"

"I think he is telling you that he will be leaving you alone but that O'nan needs careful attention."

"How is O'nan?"

"The DA made a deal that he would plead down if O'nan confessed. Save you the stress of a trial and the taxpayers' money."

"But that would mean he would get less time."

Goetz shrugged. "I just book them. I don't make the deals." He held up his hands to my protests. "I know. I know. I think it's rotten too, but the law is the law. That's something you should remember, Mrs. Reynolds."

"There's the law and then there's justice. They are not the same. And Goetz, remember, Kentuckians have a way of dispensing their own justice if the law doesn't."

"Is that a threat?"

"No, it's a promise."

26

I scream all the time.

You just can't hear me.

I scream when I try to walk and the world feels lopsided because of my limp.

I scream because I'm always having people repeat themselves because I can't hear what they're saying.

I scream because my husband walked out on me and hid his money. That's during the day. When I close my eyes at night, I dream I'm falling off that cliff again.

I scream all the way down from gut-wrenching fear.

I scream because sometimes the pain burns so intensely hot, I want to jump off that cliff again . . . and never open my eyes.

I scream because God does not answer my prayers for relief – just that pain patch, pain pills from Florida, and high-powered illegal drugs that my daughter smuggles in the country so she doesn't have to hear me cry and whimper at night when she visits.

I scream because the doctors refuse to acknowledge such intense pain or don't know how to cope with such pain or lack the guts to prescribe medication that takes care of the pain. So I am rude and disdainful; they blanch when encountering me in hallways or fumble when we're in an examination room together. That could be due to throwing my cane at a doctor who suggested that I just learn to live with the pain.

You learn to live with it, buddy.

I scream because I feel such dread that O'nan is back in Kentucky.

Even so, I had to go to the courthouse on the day of his arraignment. I watched from my car as O'nan stepped off the van, his wrists and feet shackled. He looked more powerful than when I had seen him last; his handsome facial features relaxed, giving him an appearance of calm and determination. And his eyes took in everything. He even took in my car across the street.

I did not see a man who had been humbled.

I saw a man waiting for a chance, an opportunity, a glitch so that he could act. And he would act if given a split second of the system failing. I saw a man looking for an out.

And if given that out, would he run away? Or would he come looking for me?

Yes, I scream all the time.

Wouldn't you?

27

No matter how difficult one's life is, one must get on with the business of living. So I planned Franklin's debutante party, which was going to be an old-fashioned Kentucky burgoo picnic.

Burgoo is a Kentucky stew made with venison, squirrel and rabbit, vegetables, and whiskey. Okay – the whiskey is optional, but Kentucky bourbon whiskey gives it that extra something in my opinion. I used mutton, beef, and chicken as hunting season was months away and I just didn't have lots of road kill in my freezer, dog gone it.

Based on old hunting stew recipes, burgoo is cooked for eight hours in a huge metal pot over a wood fire and stirred continuously with canoe paddles. I assigned Franklin's grumbling friends to shifts for stirring, plying them with mint juleps.

Mint juleps are also a Kentucky tradition and usually served on Derby Day. They are made with equal parts sugar and water, as much bourbon as you want served over crushed ice in chilled silver cups with sprigs of mint.

Since I had hocked all my silver julep cups for cash before my "accident," I served today's mint juleps in tasteful paper cups.

I handed one to Matt, who was in charge of the burgoo's fire and keeping the lads steadily stirring with their paddles.

"Yoo-hoo, yoo-hoo," called a lady, sprightly making her way towards us.

I squinted into the sun to see who was calling. "Who's that?" I asked.

Matt cupped his hand over his eyes. Grinning, he replied, "It's your friend. Ginny Wheelwright, I do believe."

Ginny Wheelwright was a delightful lady in her late forties who had had the misfortune of having cancer in one eye, thus having to replace it with a glass one. The problem was the eye didn't fit and this allowed Ginny to flex her muscles so that the eye would pop out, thus terrifying people. She thought it great fun.

The rest of us thought the prank in bad taste, but that didn't deter Ginny, who was going to have her practical joke.

She could also flip the eye in its socket thus confusing the person to whom she was talking. People would become hypnotized with the eye's flashing colors, only saying afterwards that they suddenly became dizzy, which is why I would not look at her face when talking to her, giving only quick glances.

Ginny gave me a quick hug. "Oh, Josiah, this is the first party you have given in seven years," she gushed. "What a treat to be invited back to the Butterfly. She looks wonderful." She glanced at Matt.

"This is my friend, Matt."

"Oh, yes, I think we've met before," simpered Ginny holding out her hand to be kissed, her eye flashing gold and then blue-white.

Amused, Matt bowed and kissed her hand, breathing, "Enchanted."

Ginny turned towards me again. "And you look wonderful too, Josiah."

I turned away. "Ginny, you gotta get that eye under control. It's making me nervous like a long-tailed cat in a room full of rocking chairs."

"Sorry, I forget," she giggled. "I mean to get a refit, but keep putting it off." Turning to Matt, Ginny confided, "Josiah and Brannon used to give the most wonderful parties." She put her hand to her mouth. "Oh, I'm sorry. I guess I shouldn't have mentioned Brannon's name."

"That's okay," I assured.

"You know Ellen is just plumb green with envy that you are back on your feet again, both literally and financially. I saw her yesterday at a luncheon and she was asking about this party. I could tell she didn't like you getting out into society again."

Ginny took out a lace handkerchief and dabbed at her brow. She turned to Matt, giving him a sly smile. "Miss

Ellen was never in the same league with our Josiah and she knows it. Just can't compete with Josiah's smarts, her good taste." She waved the handkerchief in the air for effect. "Now don't get me wrong. Ellen is a pretty little thing, but she's dumb. Oh my yes, she's dumb as a bag full of hammers, but cunning. You know the type."

I shoved a mint julep at Ginny. "Drink this, will ya, and quit yakking about Ellen."

"I guess she is still a sore spot."

"I would say so," said Matt, gently taking Ginny's hand and guiding her towards the burgoo pot.

Leading her away, I heard Matt say, "Tell me about this glorious eye of yours. The gold on its back and its reflecting light reminds me of the ancient Egyptian lighthouse – Pharos of Alexandria."

"Really?" Ginny giggled. "Now why would I want to give that up with a refit? Sounds exotic to me."

Rolling my own eyes, I turned my attention to Franklin's friends. "Keep paddling, boys. The burgoo is almost finished. Now, where's Franklin?" I asked myself.

One of the young men lowered his mint julep from his pie-hole. "He's already been here. Said he was going to give the queens a tour of the Butterfly."

"Jumping Jehosaphat, he's into my clothes," I cried, hurrying for the house. I passed the valets parking cars, hurriedly said hello to newcomers, running into Shaneika in the bamboo alcove. "Have you seen Franklin?" I asked.

Shaneika thumbed towards the house. "He's got every drag queen in the Bluegrass going through your closet."

"Merde!!!"

"Cussing in French is still cussing," admonished Mrs. Todd, following behind Shaneika.

I ran into the house, bounding into my bedroom.

Sure enough, there was Franklin pulling out my couture clothes. There were lots of ooohs as Franklin exhibited my Roberto Capucci 1982 petal sculpture dress in orange, yellow, pink, and red silk velvet. The drag queens positively clapped with glee when he showed them another Capucci dress in silk satin that resembled a geisha's formal kimono. My 1963 form fitting, strapless black sequined dress with the jutting tulle at the bottom was also a hit.

"Oh my gawd," gushed one lady impersonator. "I had a sixties Barbie with a dress just like that. Classic."

In the midst of the cacophony of rubber boobs, form-fitting dresses, wigs, and fake eyelashes sitting on my bed, lounged Lady Elsmere enjoying the show and letting her new friends try on her jewels. Her face radiated as she related the history of the dresses and to which fabulous parties I had worn them.

So June and Franklin had bumped into each other. It seemed that June had forgiven Franklin for helping Jake and me steal her pontoon boat earlier in the year.

I silently withdrew.

Franklin was handling the dresses with care and it had been years since those outfits had been admired by anybody who actually knew what they were looking at – art. Couture needs to breathe, so I decided to let everyone have a good time . . . including the clothes.

I checked on the kitchen. Charles and his grandsons had everything under control. "Charles, get out of that kitchen. You're supposed to be a guest," I admonished.

Charles grinned. "Old habits die hard. I just wanted to make sure everything was just right."

"Thank you for helping out."

"My pleasure. I see my wife is cornered by Reverend Humble. I think I will rescue her."

I smiled and opened the door for Charles while saying hello to more newcomers. After showing them to the bar and hors d'oeuvres, I saw Matt come inside with Ginny. He guided her to the bathroom and then headed straight for me.

"Something wrong?" I asked, a sinking feeling in my gut.

Looking amused, Matt replied, "That depends. I've got good news and bad news."

"What is it?"

"Ginny was telling me all about Ellen and Brannon, getting pretty excited when her eye popped out."

"Oh dear."

"The good news is we know where it is."

"Where?"

"It flew into the pot of burgoo."

"Oh no!" I gasped.

"Oh yes," Matt guffawed. "Someone is going to get a big surprise today."

"What shall we do?"

"Nothing," advised Matt, watching Ginny emerge from the bathroom with an eye patch on her left eye.

"The heat of the fire and the whiskey in the burgoo should take care of any germs. We will just look for it while we are dishing the burgoo out. Just keep mum." Matt was quiet for a moment, only to snort in the most undignified way. He flew out the door, his shoulders shaking. I could hear him laughing past the waterfall.

"I'm so sorry, Josiah," commiserated Ginny suddenly standing next to me. "It just popped out."

"I think it will be okay," I replied worriedly. I wasn't really sure.

"Can you do me a favor? If anyone finds it, can they give it back? I need it for appearance sake, you see."

"I just hope no one swallows it by mistake."

Ginny pulled out another handkerchief and blew her bulbous nose. "Now that would be a hell of a thing," she replied before tottering off toward some friends she knew.

Sighing, I turned to see Mike Connor trying to engage Shaneika in conversation. She looked bored, but tried to cover it by smiling politely.

I was sure that Mike was talking about himself. Most men think they can impress a lady with their accomplishments – big mistake in the dating area. Most people like to talk about themselves, so if a man wants to impress a woman, he should ask her questions about herself.

I took over some mint julep cups and bumped into the two of them "accidentally." "Here, have some of my famous mint juleps," I announced. "Shaneika, have you been telling Mike about your big plans for Comanche?"

I batted my eyes at Mike. "She wants to enter him in the Kentucky Derby. I bet you could help her with a winning strategy."

Mike rubbed his chin. "The Kentucky Derby, huh. Well the first thing you should do is . . ."

And with that I left the two alone while seeking out Lincoln, whom I had not seen in a while and who was not with his grandmother seated near the window with a group of similar-aged dames.

I found Lincoln, with some other boys, in my office ogling pictures in my art books. For pre-pubescent children, they were saying the most lurid things.

I snatched the textbook out of Lincoln's meaty little hands. Of course, they were gaping at Botticelli's "The Birth of Venus."

"She's naked," piped one of Lincoln's comrades.

"Yes, she is," I replied.

"She looks stupid," piped Lincoln.

"Your mother is looking for you, Lincoln," I said. And to the other conspirators, "and so are your mothers." Following them scampering out giggling, I took care to lock the office door and pocket the key. I was getting a headache and my left foot was starting to drag noticeably. I wanted a pain pill, but held off, wanting my head to be clear during the party. I could crash with one tonight.

I looked about the Butterfly. Here was an "old-school" Lexington party – old Lexingtonian aristocratic families mingling with drag queens, doctors, socialites, TV and radio personalities, poverty-stricken writers, artists, and business owners – all having a good time.

Ringing a bell, I climbed up on a chair with Franklin's help. "Dear friends," I called out. "It's so good of you to come and help welcome a dear friend of mine," I looked at Franklin standing my side, "on his debut in society. Please welcome Franklin."

Everyone cheered. Franklin beamed in his retro blue and white seersucker suit, navy blue bow tie, and straw boater hat.

Matt leaned against a wall, saluting with his mint julep, but it was obvious that he was keeping his distance.

If Franklin noticed, he didn't show it.

Some friends helped me off the chair after I directed everyone to the burgoo and a reception line where they could greet Franklin in person.

Twenty minutes later, most people were stuffing their faces with burgoo or chatting it up with Franklin. The party seemed a great success until . . .

"Oh my gawd! She's swallowed something," cried out Betty Ann Gil as Meriah Caldwell, the famous mystery writer, bent over gagging and turning red. "Help her! She's got something caught."

Matt ran over and, reaching around Caldwell's tiny waist, gave her the Heimlich maneuver.

Out popped a strange gold-looking object upon my slate floor.

Everyone gasped, except Ginny Wheelwright, who exclaimed, "You've found my eye!" Reaching down, she plucked up the glass eye, sucked it clean, and thrust it back in its socket. "Ahhh, that feels much better."

Suddenly, everyone lost their enthusiasm for my burgoo.
Go figure.

28

Since Franklin had become Lady Elsmere's, new best friend, he liked me again. All was forgiven. And he would do anything for me. So I had him do a wealth of research for me – all sorts of information about Arthur and Aspen plus lurid details about the men on Lakewood Drive.

I'm no slouch myself when it comes to research. I spent many an hour at libraries looking up information. I also contacted the UK Alumni Association and any association connected with sports. I also spent hours poring over 1961-1962 copies of the *Courier-Journal* and the *Lexington Leader*, reading articles about college sports.

I found out that Arthur was from the mountains, just like Aspen. Getting his childhood address, I visited

Arthur's home in Pike County, which has lots of millionaires.

Coal, baby, coal.

But Arthur's childhood home had been torn down. I tracked down a cousin who, persuaded by a hundred-dollar bill, confirmed that Arthur came from poor folks. His father had worked in a coal mine and his mother had been a housewife with four children to tend.

June's info was wrong. Arthur had not come from money. He had been poor growing up and had lived only several miles from Aspen as a boy. They had known each other since babyhood.

The cousin spit tobacco juice on the ground. "Excuse me," he said, pocketing the money. He got out a freshly pressed handkerchief and wiped his mouth. "Once Arthur got some money, he forgot about us at home. His mother grieved something awful."

"But how did he get his money?"

The cousin shrugged. "No one knows but during his sophomore year in college, he started flashing money around and quit the football team, losing his scholarship money."

"You're saying Arthur Greene was on a football scholarship to UK."

"Yes'am. Swear on the Bible to that."

"Then how did he pay for school after he lost his scholarship?"

The cousin shrugged again. "There were rumors that Arthur hooked up with the Chicago mob."

"Doing what? Running moonshine? Wouldn't that have put you local boys' noses out of joint?"

"Gamblin', so as I hear."

I was quiet for a moment. "Are you suggesting he was a bookie?"

"More serious."

"How serious?"

"I've said all that I'm gonna say. You figure it out, lady."

With that, he tipped his hat and went on his way.

29

I was lounging by the pool with Mrs. Todd going over some old UK football pictures when Shaneika called.

"Are you sitting?" she asked.

"Is this going to be bad?" I inquired.

"Not gonna be pleasant, Josiah. They're not throwing the book at O'nan. The judge is very sympathetic to O'nan's claims that he was suffering from stress on the job and having allergic reactions to medication."

"I thought he was going to plead guilty to lesser charges and was going to be sentenced this morning."

"There's more. Apparently there was something wrong with his extradition papers. His lawyer now is claiming that O'nan was illegally arrested in France and that the case should be dismissed on this technicality."

"I should go down there and talk to the judge."

"Don't. That will only make matters worse. I know this judge. He doesn't like a lot of emotional turmoil in his courtroom. O'nan is playing this good. He's calm, collected, and articulate. You would not be if you came down."

I had to think for a minute. I knew Shaneika was right. "What about the guy he siced on me and killed Comanche's goat?"

"That man did not identify O'nan as the man who sent him."

"He's lying."

"Yes, he is, but it's your word against his. You've no proof. Listen, I've got to go. I'll do my best to put this psycho behind bars."

Click went the phone.

I looked at my phone in dismay.

"What is it?" asked Mrs. Todd, looking alarmed. "You're white as a ghost."

"Shaneika thinks that there might be a chance that O'nan will get a light sentence or even get off."

"That can't be!" exclaimed Mrs. Todd. "That's not right."

"What's right got to do with it? We're dealing with the law."

"Oh, Lordy, say that's not true."

I poured myself a stiff bourbon.

"Hell's bells" was all I could mutter.

30

Shaneika and I were in my office discussing Arthur Greene's death. She wanted Asa to investigate, as I was getting nowhere.

"You've done your best but you've come up with nothing," stated Shaneika. "I appreciate everything you have done for Lincoln and me, but we can't stay here forever."

"Lincoln identified Arthur from my picture albums, but he never was able to identify the other man except to say that he was white, younger, and his voice sounded familiar. He just didn't get a good look at him."

"The man was too far away and it was Arthur who rushed towards him before Linc fell over the bucket. Do you think he was going to hurt Linc?" she asked.

I shook my head. "Arthur showed no signs of being a person who would hurt a child. I suppose he was startled and went to get Lincoln out of the way." I showed her the dirt-encrusted ink pen placed in a baggie. "I found this where Lincoln fell over the feeding bucket. Lady Elsmere identified it as belonging to Arthur. I think it fell out of his pocket when he was bending over trying to help Lincoln. That is when he was attacked."

"But why were you concentrating on Aspen?"

"Because it was the logical place to start. Several sources told me that things had soured between the two friends. Aspen was making demands that Arthur didn't like. But June is right about one thing. Aspen is too old and weak to have killed Arthur the way he died. Only a young, strong man or two weaker men could have hoisted that body up to the rafters."

"Maybe he hired someone."

"The murder was too full of rage. Strangling someone with a bridle. No, this was a murder of passion."

"What about a woman?"

"I doubt it. Not a woman's style at all. I still think that hanging Arthur from the rafters was symbolic. There was simply no reason for it. Arthur was already dead.
And then there were stones in his pockets and a bucket of water under him. That's ritualistic. It means something."

"Okay," surmised Shaneika. "What are the reasons people are hung?"

I tapped my fingers on the desk. "Uhmmm, people are hung because they are murderers . . . or traitors."

"Or lynched because they were black," fumed Shaneika.

"Stay focused in the present," I admonished. "This is a murder of passion, not of racial politics. People were hung after they were dead to make a point to the living. To create fear."

"Also to show disrespect of the deceased." Shaneika scratched her nose. "Didn't Judas hang himself after he betrayed Jesus?"

"Judas. Judas?" I mused. "A Judas. 'You can't tell. It will ruin me.' Which one of the men said it?"

"Obviously Arthur. He threatened the other man and so the man killed him. Maybe he was blackmailing Arthur."

I shook my head. "I have been over this man's life with a fine-tooth comb. No rumors about shady dealings. No funny bank deposits. Just a little indiscretion with our friend, June, seemed to be his only sin. Otherwise a devoted husband and father. A good business partner. Everyone liked and respected Arthur Greene. The only cloud on this man's life seem to be in 1961-62 on how he got his first money. Other than that he was clean."

"Nobody is clean," retorted Shaneika.

"Do you know anything about Freemasons?" I asked.

"Why?" Shaneika evaded.

"Because your office is in a building full of Masonic imagery. Stone in pockets and hanging over water. Might that be a Masonic ritual?"

"I have no idea," shot back Shaneika.

"When I went to talk to Kelly, he told me to look for the widow's son. That term refers to freemasonry."

"Let's stay focused on something tangible like simple greed or hate. I think my theory is right. Arthur was blackmailing someone and they got him for it." She rose from her seat. "I'm tired of thinking about this. I'm going for a swim, but afterwards I am going to call Asa."

"Okay," I agreed.

"Are you coming?"

"No, I'm going to stay here for a while and think."

Shaneika shrugged and left.

Baby, who had been sitting in the corner, rose and buried his snout in my crotch, wanting his ears scratched. I guess Lincoln was taking a nap. Absent-mindedly I rubbed Baby's ears while thinking. "Judas. Judas. Judas betrayed Jesus with a kiss. Betrayal. Betrayal. Was this a murder of revenge? It certainly was passionate enough. Was the hanging to signify that Arthur was a Judas?" I pulled Baby's head up for air. "What do you think, Baby? Was this a murder about revenge?"

Baby thumped his big head on my lap, his brown eyes looking sympathetic.

I pushed Baby off. "Hurts my leg, Baby. Go find Linc and play with him. Have him brush you."

The huge mastiff, now weighing 210 pounds, gave me a remorseful look and padded out of the room. I knew it was just an act. Baby always liked to play the martyr. A few minutes later, I spied Baby with his brush in his mouth looking for Lincoln. I guess Kelly was right. That dog was smart.

I turned back to my research on Arthur. I just knew in my gut the reason for his death stemmed from 1961-62. That was the dark cloud over Arthur's life. That was his secret.

Whom had he threaten and why?

Maybe Aspen knew.

31

The next morning I found Aspen watching Jean Harlow running Lady Elsmere's training track. I waited till she passed and Aspen clicked a stopwatch. The training jockey brought a sweating Jean Harlow back to Aspen. She was hard to control. I sensed she didn't like her rider and Aspen's instructions to hit her with a crop were unconstructive.

You don't hit a sensitive filly with a whip. You woo her. But I said nothing. Hitting with a crop was standard practice in horse racing, but I would have checked her mouth. Maybe Jean Harlow was of those horses with an overly sensitive mouth.

When Aspen turned around and saw me, he blurted out, "Aw, hell, what do you want?"

"Ms. Todd is going to call my daughter today. You know who my daughter is, don't you, Mr. Lancaster?"

Aspen blanched.

"I can see by your face you do know what she can do. If Ms. Todd hires her, my daughter will turn this town upside down in order to find out about Mr. Greene's death. There will be no secret relating to this case that she will not uncover."

"Your daughter is crazy and better stay away from me. She should be in prison."

It was my turn to blanch and then redden. "My daughter is effective and she will kick your ass if you get in her way." I smiled a gritty little smile. "Now, you can spill your guts to me, or my daughter's minions can escort you to a filthy warehouse where she will be waiting with some nasty dental tools. Ever seen the interrogation scene in *Marathon Man* with Dustin Hoffman and Laurence Olivier?" I leaned forward to whisper in his ear. "Is it safe?"

I swear he shuddered. Apparently he had seen the movie.

"Whaddya want to know?"

"Did Mr. Arthur have a secret that could have gotten him killed?"

Aspen hung his head. "Art had only one secret but I don't think it had anything to do with his death." He took deep breath before continuing.

I waited.

"Arthur and I were from the mountains and we were dirt poor. You will do anything to escape such grinding poverty if you can. Our first chance to leave those hollers and the coalfields was football scholarships. I thought

172

heaven had opened up for me with that scholarship. That is until I started the program. I had just traded one hell for another."

My left leg had started burning so I leaned heavily against the rail. I had picked a stupid place for an interview. I should have waited until he was in his office.

Aspen took no notice of my discomfort and continued. "The training was horrific and we were worked so hard that no amount of food could make up for the loss of calories. Arthur and I both lost around fifteen pounds the first six weeks and the weight kept falling off. Some of the other players liked that kind of punishment, but not me nor Arthur. The only relief we got was at Mr. Lonnie's parties."

"Parties on Lakewood Drive?"

Aspen nodded. "We were young and stupid. We just saw all that food and booze plus the pretty girls that were always there. The way we saw it, the parties were our reward for working so hard. Art and I didn't know what those men were.

"It damned near killed me when I finally realized what was going on. I hated to leave all that rich grub and those sweet young things, but leave it I did. I hated those louses for what they were."

"And Mr. Arthur?"

"He wouldn't leave. I remember standing in their driveway arguing with him. I grabbed his arm to pull him away, but he shook me off. He turned and went back. I yelled that he was going into a house of iniquity, but Art didn't seem to care."

"Do you think Mr. Arthur was gay?"

"Naw."

"What about gambling? Getting players to spread the points. That kind of thing."

Aspen shook his head. "That did not happen. I never heard anything about that. And if it had happened, it would have come out all these years."

"But rumors have persisted all these years," I argued.

"What rumors?" asked Aspen hotly.

"That college players were being bribed to throw games."

"I just told you no. Those young men were not asked to throw games and would not have if they were asked."

"Then what about Mr. Arthur?"

"I think something was said to Art to make him change. He quit the football team and lost his scholarship but suddenly found the money to finish school. Now he didn't have two nickels to throw together, so where did he get money?"

I waited saying nothing.

"We had it out one night. No matter what, Art was from my hometown. I was gonna look out for him if I could. I asked him where he got the money. Art just laughed, saying instead of those old queens using him, he was using them. I asked what he meant by that, but he wouldn't tell me.

"Things finally came to a head about those men. The older teammates went to Coach Bradshaw and told him the going-ons at their house. The Coach had the police throw those rascals out of town, but everything was hushed up."

"What happened then?"

"Art had more money than ever. In fact, he invested a thousand dollars for me in the stock market. The money made from that was my startup money. He just did it without my knowledge and gave me a wad of money one day. I know I shouldn't have taken it, but I was desperate. I'm no better than Art. Money to a poor boy is a huge temptation. But you can see why I will always be beholden to Art for what he did for me and in return I have kept his secret all these years."

"And clear that up for me again."

Aspen looked at me like I was a dunce. "Art was the go-between. He was the one to actually approach young players and recruit them for parties on Lakewood Drive. Art was told when and he would make it happen. That way, those two men never got their hands dirty. Art brought young men to them."

"Do you think that had anything to do with his getting killed?"

Aspen scratched his balding head. "I don't know. I keep going over in my head who hated Art enough to strangle him, but I can't come up with one name. Everyone liked Art. He was good to people. After that episode as a young man, Arthur turned into a straight arrow. There was not a dime that he had that wasn't honest and he never took advantage of anyone's naivety again. I'll swear to that on the Bible."

"Was he faithful to his wife? Do you think he might have had an affair?"

"Oh, hell no. I told you Art was a straight arrow. A regular church-goer."

I didn't think Aspen could tell me any more. He didn't know about June and Mr. Arthur's affair. He didn't know his childhood friend, Arthur Greene, as well as he thought he did.

"Just one more thing. Did you kill Mr. Arthur?"

Aspen's face turned red. "If you were a man, I knock you down. Now git and don't come back."

Since his hands were balled into fists at his side, I took his advice.

I know when I'm not wanted.

32

Doodling on my yellow legal pad, I couldn't come up with a theory about Arthur Greene's death. People murder for money, passion, and revenge. Arthur had been on the up-and-up for over 40 years when it came to money, so I ruled that out. So it had to be either sex or revenge.

Could Arthur's wife, Lucinda, have found out about June? Could a woman in her sixties be so incensed about her husband's affair that she would kill him? I knew she couldn't have killed him herself, but Lucinda could have hired someone. This is not uncommon in the state of Kentucky.

Maybe Arthur had had a string of affairs and she finally just snapped. It was worth looking into.

I thought back to when I realized that my husband, Brannon, was having an affair with an acquaintance of mine. I had been mad enough to kill. I hated him for his betrayal and hated his girlfriend.

Hmmm. Was Lady Elsmere in danger? I made a note on the legal pad to discuss that issue with Charles. No use talking to June as she had only three subjects of discussion – jewels, horses, and the past. And those dinner parties!

Thinking again of Lucinda Greene, I would have to accidentally bump into her. As we knew each other just to say hello, I couldn't very well call her up or drop by.

"This must be done delicately," said the *Wicked Witch of the West.*

I snapped my fingers. I knew the way. June was a member of the Fayette Matrons Club, which was a meeting place for moneyed, aristocratic women with a southern viewpoint to meet and espouse their outdated views without being called bigots by the rest of the world. Lucinda ate there three times a week.

I called June and got her to make a reservation on my behalf. She wanted to come but I discouraged this. No matter how well behaved June was, there was bound to be tension between the two women after June had acted like a fool at Arthur's funeral. And I am sure that Lucinda would be brimming with questions. If she did not formerly know about Arthur and June's close relationship she was now sure to be suspicious that something was up.

The reservation was made for Wednesday. It gave me a day to have my hair done, eyebrows waxed, and nails polished. After my makeover in Key West, I tried to keep up with my grooming since it pleased Matt so. Wearing a simple black dress with a heavy silver Navaho necklace, I entered an alleyway and knocked on a discreetly carved door. An African-American butler wearing white gloves opened it. I told him that I was Lady Elsmere's guest for the day. He nodded and opened the door wider to let me enter.

The foyer was papered in yellow and white striped wallpaper from the late seventies and the painted white furniture was covered in yellow velour upholstery with some potted elephant ears in the corners. On the main wall behind a massive desk was a picture of Robert E. Lee in full Confederate uniform sitting on a white horse. On the opposite wall proudly hung a Confederate battle flag, dirty and black with soot and blood. It looked like the real thing.

The butler watching my expression just smiled.

"Why?"

He shrugged. "Good benefits," he whispered as he showed me to my table.

Apparently Lady Elsmere had clout as I was seated at a table near one of the few windows in the place. The candle on the table was lit and a vase with a fresh yellow rose was moved to the middle. My glass was filled with water and bread immediately brought by one of the many black staff that scurried to wait on their white patrons whom I studied out of the corner of my eyes.

All the women were white, middle-aged or older. All had that old-money look about them – shoulder-length or shorter hair in various shades of blond or silver-gray, expensive skirts or pantsuits in various shades of navy, beige or white, small gold earrings accompanied by family brooches. All wore expensive wristwatches. No cell phones on the table.

The chattering was low as many were eating by themselves. They didn't look lonely. Maybe they came here to have a few moments by themselves, away from demanding husbands, clamorous charity boards, and irksome kids.

Speaking of food, my stomach growled. I glanced at the menu. As soon as I put it down, a waiter was by my side. I told him I wanted the salmon.

He asked if I wanted to wait for Lady Elsmere.

I lied and said that she had called saying that she couldn't make it. He nodded and made for the kitchen.

Taking a sip of my water, I studied Lucinda Greene seated not too far from me. I gave her a few moments to settle in before I launched my attack. As she was looking in her purse, I limped over with my cane.

"Lucinda." I acted surprised to see her.

"Josiah," she responded. "How nice to see you." Lucinda blinked several times.

"I didn't get a chance to speak to you at the funeral."

Lucinda interrupted. "Yes, that was quite a spectacle June put on."

"Uhmmm, she had been taking a strong medication and I think it backfired on her – just at the most unfortunate time," I responded, trying to cover up for June. "In fact, I was supposed to meet her here, but she called saying she didn't feel well."

Lucinda nodded.

"I mean she is very old. Eighty-eight, I think." I paused for a moment, waiting for her to ask me to sit down but she didn't, so I rambled on. "Anyway I wanted to express my condolences."

She nodded again.

I winced as though my leg was hurting me. "I've got to sit down. This leg is killing me." Hint. Hint.

Nothing. Lucinda just smiled at me in superficial sympathy.

"Perhaps you would like to join me, Lucinda, since June isn't coming."

I could tell she was about to decline, so I blurted out, "I so hate to eat alone." I leaned on my cane looking pitiful.

Sighing, she threw down her napkin and reluctantly rose. "Of course. It would be a pleasure," Lucinda lied.

A waiter immediately appeared out of nowhere and escorted Lucinda to my table, holding a chair out for her. Another waiter brought her purse and placed it in a vacant chair.

Happy at my success, I lit her cigarette, which she retrieved from a silver case. Apparently this club ignored the smoking ban in Lexington. She inhaled deeply. No lung cancer fears for Lucinda. She laughed when she saw my questioning face.

"My one vice," she quipped.

"Only one? You must be a saint."

"I never could break the habit."

An ashtray appeared immediately on the table. One thing about this place, it had great service.

"This is the first time I've eaten here."

Lucinda took another drag. "It's mostly old bags like myself with lots of money to throw around, but I like it," she responded, smoke spilling out of her nose. "I come here to have some time to myself. The food is outstanding. No one hassles me. Cell phones are forbidden. It's my little oasis."

"Nice. Who owns it?"

"I do, honey child." Lucinda removed a bit of tobacco from her bottom lip. "I bought it six years ago. I just wanted a place to go to. You know. Have a drink. Read the paper and have a nice lunch."

I nodded.

"The place was a shambles when I bought it. You should have seen it."

"I never see any advertisements."

Lucinda gave me a look of horror. "We don't need to. It's a private club. Word of mouth only. In fact we have a waiting list."

I noticed that I was never invited to join but I let that thought pass as our food was served. My pecan-crusted salmon on a bed of garlic mashed potatoes melted in my mouth. Lucinda had a small salad accompanied by vegetable rice dish. We dove in and didn't come up for air for several minutes.

"How are you coping?" I asked between bites.

Lucinda's face fell, giving her a deer in the headlights appearance. "Since you are a widow too, I know you understand. I still expect him to come through the door.

This entire mess of Arthur's death is dreadful. Just dreadful."

"Any leads?"

"That's the frustrating part. Everyone liked Arthur. He didn't have any enemies."

"What about kinfolk from the mountains or someone from his past."

"How did you know that Arthur was from Eastern Kentucky?" She answered her own question. "Ah, June. She would have told you. She and Arthur were quite close, you know."

"I didn't know that. I just thought he gave her financial advice."

Lucinda nodded. "He did that too. Arthur was good with money." She waved her hand. "Look around. He gave financial advice to most of the women here."

"How did Arthur make his money?" I asked innocently as I took another bite of my salmon.

"Arthur inherited it. His father was in coal."

"Oh, really. Did you ever meet his family?"

"No. They were deceased by the time I met Arthur."

"Ahh," I responded knowing that Arthur's father had worked in the coalmines as a miner. He had been dirt poor.

"For some reason I thought Arthur had a football scholarship to UK," I mused.

Lucinda shook her head. "No, no. Arthur was on the football team for only one season before he hurt his knee, but his friend Aspen was on a scholarship."

"I see."

She sighed. "Josiah, may I confide something to you?"

"You can trust me."

"I never understood what Arthur saw in Aspen. They were not of the same social or financial class, but those two were thick as thieves."

"Aspen is hard to take in large dosages."

"He is indeed, but he was at my house every holiday and any televised UK football game watching with Arthur." She paused for a second. "But I must tell you that he as been good as gold since Arthur was killed. He seems really devastated."

"Uh huh."

"In fact, he offered to cut me in on Jean Harlow."

"Did you take him up on it?"

"Oh, heavens no. I don't want to spend time with Aspen and I don't like going to the races. In fact, after this mess with Arthur is solved, I'm going to move to Palm Beach. I've had enough of Kentucky."

"Lucinda, who do you think murdered Arthur?"

She blinked again. "I really don't know. I really don't. It's a total mystery to me who killed that sweet man."

"I don't want to offend you, but maybe he had a sweetie on the side who wanted him dead or maybe he owed money to a shark."

Lucinda laughed. "I can assure you that Arthur was as faithful as a man can be and as for a loan shark, well, our children and I will be well provided for. No, Josiah, it was a drifter or someone who was crazy. It was not one of our own who did this."

I felt Lucinda was sincere. She loved her husband and thought him blameless in his own death. And she didn't have a clue about June. Lucinda was a sharp woman, which told me that Arthur was very good at deception and manipulation. Yes. Arthur had many secrets. He was not the good egg everyone thought he was.

I quit asking questions. There was nothing more to find out. I mentally scratched Lucinda off my suspect list.

Suddenly I felt tears in my eyes. I felt very sorry for Lucinda Greene. I hoped no one ever told her the truth, but I knew it would all come out eventually. Then her kind vision of her husband would be trampled and this nice woman would be devastated for the rest of her life.

All men are bastards.

33

Are all men bastards? I really didn't think so, at least, deep down. Just on the surface. Kindness and understanding is inherent in both sexes.

Take Franklin for instance.

I was writing down the information I had gleaned at this afternoon's luncheon when Franklin appeared at my office door. I waved him in.

Still writing, I asked, "Well, Franklin, any invitations from the party?"

"Oodles," he responded. "And I'm invited to Lady Elsmere's house next Saturday for tea. I think I am her new BFF."

"No doubt," I replied looking up from my notes. "You got what you wanted."

"And you got what you wanted, missy."

"What does that mean?" Fear shot through my heart.

Franklin laid a red hair with golden highlights on my notepad.

I said nothing.

"I found this in Matt's shower."

"So?"

"So — when did you sleep with Matt?"

"Don't be insane, Franklin."

"I know what I know. Don't lie to me, Josiah."

"What this means is that Matt washed off one of my hairs. He is around here all the time. It is very easy for one of my hairs to get on him."

He pointed a finger at me. "There has always been tension between the two of you and now, all of a sudden the tension is gone. I know what I know."

"Jumping Jehosaphat, Franklin," I blustered, lowering my eyes. There was no way I was going to get out of this. I had to fess up. "It was my fault. I pushed the issue. I was beside myself, missing Jake. I just didn't want to spend another night alone. It was a one-time thing only. Matt made that very clear."

Franklin sighed with relief. "Since you two had your little tryst, Matt has been an absolute doll to me. I guess it's the guilt. He is nothing but sweet like summer peach juice these past weeks. My life has been a joy, so I will forgive you."

"I'm so sorry Franklin. Really I am. It was a case of me being weak and Matt being kind."

Franklin leaned over the desk to look me squarely in the eye. "I'll hurt you, Josiah, if you try to take Matt away from me. I give you fair warning."

I stared back. "I understand, Franklin."

He leaned back. "So?"

"So what?"

"How was my boy?"

I answered truthfully. "He was the best. I expected no less."

"That's my boy. Home run every time," Franklin boasted proudly. "And Josiah?"

"Yeah?"

"I know all about those other women Matt sees. They don't mean a thing. I think Matt is trying to prove something to himself, but Matt will always be drawn to the gay lifestyle no matter how hard he may try to be heterosexual. He is essentially a gay man."

"I know."

"You're something different though."

"I know."

"You understand me?"

"Loud and clear."

"You're feeling me?" he said, snapping his fingers.

"Yes sir."

"We on the same page?"

"Franklin. This is starting to wear me down."

"Okay girlfriend. Just want to make sure there are no misunderstandings."

"You must love Matt a lot."

Franklin looked out the patio door. "Girlfriend, you have no idea how much I love that man. I would die for him."

And Franklin almost did, but that would come much, much later.

34

I reviewed my list of suspects. They were dwindling fast.

Lucinda: Crossed her off.

Children: Crushed by daddy's death.

Aspen: I didn't think he had anything to do with it; besides he was too old.

June: Jealous. Could have hired someone but I didn't think so.

Random serial killer: Unlikely.

Loan shark: Nope. Finances were in impeccable order.

Pissed-off client: Not a whisper of such a disgruntled person.

Football buddies: Why now after all these years? Besides they were ancient like Aspen.

The only blemish on Arthur's life was 1962, and of course, June.

I was stumped.

I called Goetz and asked him about the case.

He hung up on me.

I called again and asked him out to dinner – no questions asked. I was desperate for company, even his. Goetz made me promise not to ask about the case. I was hoping he would let breadcrumbs of information fall sometime during dinner.

We met at Columbia's, a steak house, that evening. I ordered the special and a baked potato with all the trimmings. Goetz ordered the same plus a couple of drinks for us. I hoped the booze would loosen his tongue.

"Goetz, you ever married?"

"Divorced. Lives in Charleston, South Carolina, alone. Her boyfriend ran out on her. I told her he was no good but she never listened to me."

"Gonna take her back?"

Goetz looked at me surprised. "No. Besides, she left years ago. Stranger now."

"Kids?"

"Two. Grown. Both married and live out of state. Both in the medical profession."

I could tell he was proud of them. Goetz got out his wallet and showed a picture of them. They were good-looking kids smiling with their dad, his arm around each of them.

"You miss being married?"

I nodded. "I don't like living alone."

"What happened?"

"Brannon, that's my husband, drifted in a different direction, I guess. To tell you the truth, I thought we were happy. His affair took me by surprise. I just wasn't paying attention."

"Doesn't sound like you – not paying attention. Maybe your husband was just a sneaky son-of-a-gun."

I took a sip of my whiskey sour. "It turns out he was, but it sure threw me for a loop. And then he had a heart attack after we had a big fight. He died several days later. It was too horrible for words, but the worst came afterwards. Brannon hid money and Ellen, that's his girlfriend, got the bulk of his estate. I just can't prove it."

I took another sip. "He must have really hated me to do that. He didn't even leave his only daughter a farthing."

Goetz's droopy face folded into a sympathetic façade. "Gee, that's rotten."

I took another sip. "You bet it is." I motioned to the waiter for another drink. Wait a minute! Who was trying to get whom drunk?

"No one since your wife?"

"I've dated a little bit, but nothing serious."

I nodded. "I thought you were going to retire?"

"I've got eleven months to go. Counting every day."

"What do you have planned?"

Goetz buttered a roll and pulled off a piece. "Read. Watch movies. Learn how to swim."

"You don't know how to swim?"

"Nope, but gonna learn before I die."

"Why don't you come to the house? I'll teach you to swim. I'm a very good swimmer. Taught my daughter to swim."

Goetz gazed at me like a puppy about to receive a new ball, and then his cop face pushed the other out. Changing the subject, he asked, "Where's your bodyguard, Jake?"

"Asa reassigned him after O'nan was caught."

"Didn't he help you with your therapy?"

"I'm well enough to finish on my own."

Goetz took a bit of his steak dripping with garlic butter. He took another bite before he asked, "I hear you've been poking around the Greene case."

"I thought we weren't going to talk about that. You know Ms. Todd asked me to look into it. She said she is going to bring Asa into it if the case doesn't break soon."

"Is she that tired of your cooking?"

"Ha. Ha."

Goetz wiped his mouth off. "Don't bring your daughter into this. It will do nothing but screw things up."

"Are you close?"

"Getting there."

"Anything you would like to tell me?"

He gave me a cheesy grin. "Shaking a tree loose of fruit here and there."

"Anything kinky?" I quizzed, holding my breath that he did not mention Lady Elsmere.

"Naw, the guy was a straight arrow," Goetz replied. "Do you know something?"

"I'm like you – stuck," I replied.

"Now that we've gotten that out of the way, let's talk about other things," Goetz said.   "I heard through the grapevine that your FBI buddy, Larry Bingham, is in Arizona with Tellie Pidgeon."

I leaned back in my chair. "Well, I'll be. I was right after all."

"Right about what?"

"How Richard Pidgeon really died."

Goetz tapped the table forcibly with his fingers. "That case is closed and I never want you to mention it to me again. If it weren't for you sticking your nose in it, you wouldn't be walking like a gimp with a stick and going 'huh?' after everything I say."

Stunned at his sudden anger, I sat looking at him for almost a minute. Then gathering my wits, I retrieved my purse and threw twenty bucks on the table. "Sometimes Goetz, you're the crudest man I've ever met." I gave him a withering look. "You get to leave the tip, jerk."

I went home, had some hot chocolate, and slept the sleep of the dead.

The next morning, Goetz called me.

I hung up.

He called me again.

I hung up.

Called again.

Hung up.

Hung up.

Hung up.

35

Not so long ago, buffalo roamed Kentucky. Five hundred thousand giant, prehistoric-looking, hump-backed bison thundered across the Bluegrass; their sharp hooves beating permanent traces into the earth on their way to the salt licks like Big Bone and Blue Lick, paving the way for humans to follow their massive trails. The Native Americans used the pathways as trading routes and then as military roads going back and forth from Ohio into Kentucky and Virginia. It was the buffalo traces that the Europeans followed out West, chasing after dreams of gold, land, and glory.

The number of bison across North America was incalculable, but humans almost wiped them out anyway. There are now fewer than sixty registered buffalo herds in Canada and the United States, with Ted Turner owning twenty percent of them. They were once the dominant animals – now they are fewer than the hairs on my head.

I can quite imagine their surprise about being displaced. It must have been a similar surprise when Shaneika showed up in my beeyard during the middle of the day in her high heels and business suit.

"You best quit and come on back to the house. I need to talk to you," she yelled from a distance.

I didn't like this one bit. Closing the hive I had been working, I put the smoker on top of it and poured water in its belching tube. Darn – it had really been putting out the smoke too. Getting the smoker to work correctly was the hardest thing about beekeeping.

Jumping into my electric cart, I sped over to Shaneika and picked her up.

"Let's go to Matt's house. He's waiting for us," she said in her British clip.

I didn't say a word but I knew it had to be bad. When we got to Matt's little bungalow, he was waiting for us with a pitcher of lemonade and a bottle of Kentucky bourbon. His coat was off with his shirtsleeves rolled up. His silk tie was loosened and a lock of black hair fell on his forehead. The sight of him made my heart skip a beat.

Taking off my beekeeper's veil and suit, I threw them in the back of the cart. I hobbled up the three short steps to the porch and, taking a seat, accepted lemonade from Matt. I poured some bourbon in it and took a long draw.

Shaneika did the same sitting across from me while Matt leaned against the porch railing.

"Okay, give it to me," I admonished. "What's wrong?"

"The judge has let O'nan out on bail."

I blurted out, "You gotta be kidding me!" I started to wheeze. Matt held out an inhaler for me, which I gratefully accepted. I always forgot to keep inhalers with me but Matt always had one on hand.

Shaneika shook her head. "I am as disgusted as you are but here's what happened. France has no extradition treaty with the U.S. Interpol picked O'nan up and held him in a French jail waiting for a U.S. Marshal to retrieve him. He was never formally charged but he sat there for days waiting and was questioned by the French police. His lawyer is making the case that O'nan was kidnapped by a foreign power and his civil rights were violated, as he was never charged with a crime.

"Then the U.S. Marshal did not mirandize O'nan when he picked him up. That again was a violation of the law. He wasn't mirandize until he was put in jail in Lexington."

Shaneika waved her hand, exasperated. "The District Attorney argued and argued with that judge, but the judge says that O'nan was a decorated police officer and nothing was amiss until the Pidgeon case. O'nan says that you accosted him sexually at Pidgeon's funeral near the downstairs church bathroom and you unduly made misleading complaints against him."

"How does he explain shooting Franklin and throwing me off a cliff?"

"His lawyer explained that O'nan was there in an official capacity and that you attacked and pushed him off the cliff. You lost your balance and fell. As for Franklin, O'nan claims he was only acting in self-defense."

I cradled my head. "This is a nightmare. Does the judge really believe this bull?"

Matt interceded, "I watched the proceeding. That DA did everything in her power to convince the judge that O'nan was crazy, but that man is very pro-police and I just don't think he likes this case, Josiah."

"When Job asked God why he had cursed him— killing his family, his cattle, taking his wealth away, and causing great injury to his body when Job so loved him – you know what God replied?"

Matt shook his head.

""There is something about you, Job, that just pisses me off,'" I replied.

I took the bourbon bottle and took a big swig. "So now what?" I asked, wiping my chin off with my sleeve.

Shaneika responded, "I am going to request another judge. Do you know this guy? His name is Thaddeus Reveal."

I shook my head. "The name is not familiar to me."

Matt intercepted. "Perhaps he knows Ellen."

"I never thought of that," responded Shaneika, writing herself a note. "I'll have it checked out."

"What else?" I asked. "There is always a what else."

"If O'nan wins, the city will want their money back."

"This gets better and better." I stood. "There is nothing I can do about this tonight. You all come out to the house to eat. Everyone thinks better on a full stomach."

"Franklin's coming," Matt stated.

"We'll set another place," I said. "One more won't hurt. Besides this will affect him too. Does he know?"

Matt winced. "I broke it to him a couple of hours ago."

"And?"

"He got very quiet. Didn't say much. I don't like it," said Matt.

"It does kind of take your breath away," I stated. "Come on down when you're ready. I am sure Mrs. Todd has something wonderful for us to eat tonight."

"I called Mom. She said crispy fried catfish with gravy, pickled green beans, spoon bread, buttered corn on the cob, red beets, and cold, sour cream potato salad with herbs. And lemon cake with marshmallow icing for dessert."

"You see," I said. "Life is already looking up."

Since Jake had left, I had been regaining weight but right now I didn't give a flip. I was going to eat until I was stuffed and someone had to roll me to bed.
The only thing I knew to do was to go forward so I hired Mrs. Todd as my cook that night.

After this murder mess was over, she would return twice a week and cook plus do light housekeeping. She needed something to occupy herself to feel useful and needed.

I was doing the needing.

36

Goetz didn't like the setup one bit. For one thing, he was out of his jurisdiction. If anything happened, he would have no authority over the situation. It was also near one in the morning. With few lights in the area, one misstep could plunge him hundreds of feet down into the Kentucky River. Why had he agreed to this meeting at High Bridge of all places?

The bridge stood ominous against a dark sky with clouds occasionally moving out of a waning moon's way, creating deeper shadows. Built in 1911 by Gustav Lindenthal around an older bridge designed by John Roebling in 1876, the structure had been the tallest bridge above a navigable waterway.

Wind moaned through its beams. It looked powerful, wicked, and immune to the plights of the humans who lived below it. Goetz didn't like the bridge one bit.

He stepped out of his car, acclimating his eyes to the dark. Just the lights of houses thousands of feet away in the valley across the river and a few lights on the bridge shone. *Just pinpoints in the black.*

A lonely train whistled in the distance. Oh great! A train was coming that would rattle across the bridge creating stronger winds. Comforted by the feel of a small gun in his pocket, Goetz slowly turned 360 degrees looking for his contact.

"*Guten abend, Goetz,*" *whispered a figure stepping out of the shadows.*

"*You've been watching me?*"

"*You've lost weight.*"

"*Whaddya want, Fred?*"

"*Just a chance to clear things up.*"

"*I can't believe that you were let out on bail. Unbelievable. That judge must have rocks in his head.*"

"*Maybe he knows a cop that's been wronged when he sees one.*"

"*I'll be testifying for the District Attorney. You screwed up. That doesn't change.*"

O'nan grinned. "*I don't think so. I'm going to get off scot-free.*" *He laughed.*

Goetz's fingers closed around the gun's trigger. He said nothing.

"*You see, Goetz, I was an informant for the FBI. Yeah, I can see that surprises you. Larry Bingham was my contact for years.*"

"*Don't piss on my leg and tell me it's raining. He was retired when you started this crap with Josiah Reynolds. Can you really hate her this much? I mean, come on boy, you have always been a screw-up. You can't blame her for you being an idiot.*"

O'nan's smile faltered. "*Don't call me names. I don't like that.*"

It was Goetz's turn to smile. "*That's why I do it.*"

"*I wouldn't insult me.*" *O'nan began to unbutton his jacket.*

201

Immediately Goetz thrust his coat up with his hand in his pocket. "Don't!"

O'nan grinned again. "A gun in your pocket? Tsk. Tsk. I was just going for some cigarettes." O'nan pulled out a pack of Camels. He offered a cigarette to Goetz, who shook his head. "Now let's get back to why you should not insult me. You are going to be a hostile witness for the prosecutor and . . ."

Goetz guffawed.

"And you are going to help set me free."

"You must be dreaming, son."

O'nan continued, "Because if you don't, it is going to be conveyed to your offspring that their college was paid with kickbacks from the Cornbread Mafia. What, no snappy comeback? I can see by your face you didn't know that I knew." O'nan lit his cigarette. "Larry gave me a thick file on you. Oh, yeah, you were being investigated for corruption by the ATF, but then the head honcho of the Cornbread Mafia killed his wife and well . . . there were other priorities."

O'nan flicked ashes on the ground. "But there are still the photographs of you taking payoffs for letting truckloads of marijuana and bootlegged cartons of cigarettes travel up our beloved I-75 into Ohio. I guess you were to tip them off in case the state cops or the ATF got too inquisitive." He shook his head. "Now who are you to call me a bad boy when you've been so nasty yourself." O'nan grinned again. "You make sure that you testify the right way or your little girl is going to be crying her eyes out when she finds out about her corrupt daddy."

"How did Bingham get his hands on those ATF files?"

"When I started working with you as a partner, I asked him to check you out. He knew a guy who had a buddy in the state police and the ATF. The ATF came through."

"I ought to throw you off this cliff."

"Done that and sooooo over it. You won't kill me, buddy boy. Taking bribes is one thing but murdering . . . not your style at all."

"Maybe I won't have to. I hear Asa Reynolds might come to town soon, and we both know what a short trigger she has on her temper. She's not hired by the big guns for her moral nature."

"Her mother shouldn't have messed with me."

"You thought you could take revenge on Reynolds because she was down on her luck and alone. It never occurred to you that her little girl would grow up to play such hardball. How much money do you think she spent on tracking you down? If you hurt her mother again, Asa Reynolds will spend her last dime, her last breath on getting you and you won't be turned over to the police the next time. She will take care of you herself."

O'nan yawned. "I didn't know that you were such a drama queen. Just worry about yourself and the kiddies. If I go down, so do you. Remember that." O'nan waved goodbye. "See ya in court," said O'nan's, his voice trailing off as he disappeared into the dark.

Goetz broke out into a cold sweat. He was trapped like a raccoon up a tree with a determined Bluetick Coonhound bounding down below. Leaning against his car, he took out his handkerchief and wiped his face. He didn't want to betray Josiah Reynolds. He liked her, respected her — maybe even wanted her. What was he going to do now?

37

I was in my office listening to *Lakmé* by Delibes when Linc sashayed in holding one kitten with another riding on his head. The other two he had placed on the back of Baby, who followed obediently behind. His free hand wasn't free at all, but held a tuna salad sandwich, which was dribbling tiny bits of tuna on my clean floor. The kittens on Baby immediately jumped down and cleaned it up – literally. The other kittens meowed in distress, as they were not able to join in the gleaning.

"Linc, you're dropping your sandwich on the floor," I admonished.

Lincoln looked down. Grinning, he took a big bite and leaned against my desk, looking at all the pictures I had laid out.

I rescued the poor kitten off his head along with the one Lincoln was holding and put them on the floor, where they scampered trying to cash in on the fallen tuna.

Baby rested his head on the desk as well, snorting a huge sigh.

I sighed as well, wiping off Baby's goo with some paper towels I always kept by the desk. He nuzzled my arm in thanks and then licked his entire face, dispensing more dripping slobber.

"Hey, guys, you're getting stuff all over these pictures." I pushed Baby's massive head off the desk.

Lincoln took another bite of his sandwich while leaning over in my light to see the pictures.

"Linc, you're blocking the light!"

The boy shifted just a bit before he began rearranging the pictures with a clean finger – the one he had put in his mouth, sucked clean, and wiped on his pants.

I groaned, having forgotten how kids were. "Linc, I think I hear your mother calling."

Lincoln cocked his head straining to listen. "Nope. I don't hear anything." He picked up a couple of pictures, looking at them intently.

"Linc, you're still in my light. I can't see."

"Unhuh," he mumbled while picking up another picture. He dropped that one and began studying a team picture of the 1962 UK football team before so many members left. Making a soft ummph sound, he put the picture closer to his eyes.

"What is it, Linc?"

"This man is Mr. Slade." Lincoln turned the picture so I could see to where he was pointing.

"You mean Mr. Slade who is the manager of the Royal Blue Stables?"

"Yeah, that's him. That's him."

I looked at the picture and then the legend with the player's names. It said Daniel Slade for the player in the back row. Taking out a magnifying glass, I studied the image. I had seen Dan Slade only once but this sure looked like him.

"This can't be Mr. Slade. It was taken in the summer of 1962. See? But this might be his father."

"Look," he said pointing to Arthur Greene's image. "That's one of the men I saw arguing in the barn that night. He looks real young here but that was him."

I nodded in agreement.

"And this man," he said, pointing to Daniel Slade. "He looks like the other man but the man I saw was older, bigger, not so thin."

"Lincoln, you never said that Dan Slade was there that night. What makes you say that now?"

Lincoln shrugged. "Didn't remember. Seeing the picture brings it back."

"Lincoln, are you really sure or just guessing? Now tell the truth. This is very important."

Lincoln shifted uneasily and would not lock eyes with me. "I don't know. I must be wrong."

I had scared him. "Okay, Linc. Why don't you get ready for bed."

Lincoln grinned and ran off with Baby right behind him and the kittens scampering right behind Baby.

I gazed at the picture. Was Lincoln right? Did he just now remember that the other man was Daniel Slade Jr., obviously the son of a Daniel Slade who played on the

1962 UK football team? Four players to the left stood Arthur Greene with Aspen in the front row.

With the picture in tow, I knocked on Mrs. Todd's bedroom door. She was in bed reading a magazine. "What is it, Josiah?" she said in a quiet voice that dripped like warm honey.

I showed her the picture and what Lincoln had said.

"I think it's time to go see Leon again," I stated.

38

"To what do I owe this pleasure again?" rasped Leon, looking frailer than when we had last seen him. "Jimmy, get these ladies a Coca-Cola with lots of ice. It's so hot."

Mrs. Todd and I signaled no. I handed Leon the 1962 team picture. "Mr. Short, can you tell us anything about Daniel Slade?"

Leon held the picture very close to his eyes. "Oh my goodness, this brings back such memories. My. My. It does my heart good to see these young fellers again."

"Daniel Slade?" I reminded.

"Yes, Danny. He was a very good receiver."

"Was he a regular at Mr. Lonnie's house?"

Leon nodded. "Oh my yes. He loved the ladies who came to the parties. He was a particular favorite of Mr. Lonnie's."

"Was he involved in any illicit pursuits?"

"Huh?"

Mrs. Todd leaned forward. "Was he up to no good with those men?"

Leon paused for a moment. "There were rumors that he was one of the players who was enticed with money."

"To do what?"

"To come to the parties."

"For what purpose?"

Leon just shrugged. "Mr. Lonnie liked dark-haired men."

Mrs. Todd and I looked at each other. I just got a sinking feeling in my stomach.

"And no authority figure stepped in and stopped these parties?" asked Mrs. Todd.

"Like I told ya before, it never came up as no one suspected until later when my employers were asked to leave town."

"Never in the papers?"

"Not a word. Things were different back then, but only a handful of people really knew anything for sure. The rest of us just guessed what was coming down with certain players. How else could they afford new cars and throw money all around town?"

"What do you think?"

"What do I think? I think Mr. Danny was dirty as hell."

I glanced at Mrs. Todd.

"Now wait a moment before you women get your skirts in a knot," cautioned Leon, half rising from his chair. "Folks were very poor back then. You did what you could to get by. Don't you go judging. The college paid for their room and board, but made them work like mules for rich white folks with their new Cadillacs and fancy sports clothes coming to watch these boys like they were gladiators in Rome. Those people just wanted to be entertained and feel like they were big shots. They didn't give a damn if those boys got enough to eat or were treated bad or got hurt. They used those boys like pimps use whores. Still do. No, don't you go judging Danny Slade," he admonished, pointing a frail finger at us. "You do what you have to do to get by in this world."

He called to Jimmy. "Bring me those pictures." Turning to us, he said, "I asked my daughter to help me find some pictures." Jimmy dropped a baggie with photographs in Leon's lap. Fumbling with the catch, he finally opened the plastic bag and dumped them on his afghan. Carefully he went through each one until he came to one he wanted. Leon handed it to me.

It was of Arthur and Daniel Slade raising beer bottles to the camera and smiling with all the vigor and happiness that youth can afford.

"Those two were thick as thieves for a while. Then things went sour between them." Leon leaned back in his easy chair while wrapping his afghan tighter around him. "I had to break up a fight between them one time. Mr. Danny was yelling that Mr. Arthur owed him money."

"What did Mr. Arthur do?"

"He was right disturbed. Kept trying to reason with Mr. Danny, saying that Mr. Danny didn't follow instructions so there was no money to be had. Mr.

210

Danny said he had risked everything and it wasn't over until he got his. Mr. Arthur said there was no reasoning with a fool and walked away."

"What happened then?"

"Mr. Danny swore an oath of revenge. I ain't ever seen any man so mad as him. It right scared me so I let him go and told Mr. Lonnie about it. Mr. Lonnie said he would talk to Mr. Danny about it. That's the last I heard of it except that later on, Mr. Aspen and Mr. Danny had gone into business together and bought the Royal Blue Stables."

"Aspen owned the Royal Blue?"

"They both did until they lost it. People say it was Mr. Danny that was responsible. Not a good businessman. Some people are good with money and some ain't."

Neither Mrs. Todd nor I breathed, fearing Leon would stop talking.

"That's when Mr. Aspen asked for a loan to tide them over, but Mr. Arthur wouldn't because of hard feelings against his partner, Mr. Danny. It was like Mr. Arthur wanted them to fail.

"When they both lost the Royal Blue Farm, the stress became so bad that Mr. Danny had a heart attack and died right on the spot."

"Then what happened?"

"After that, Mr. Arthur got Mr. Aspen jobs and took him on himself. Got him back on his feet financially."

"When did Mr. Danny die?"

Leon scratched his chin. "About 1991, 92, somewhere in there. I know that his children were still at home."

I was furiously taking notes. "Leon, where did Mr. Danny die?"

Leon looked at me like I was kind of stupid. "At the exact spot that Mr. Arthur was killed, according to the pictures in the paper."

I stopped writing. I knew who the killer was, but proving it was going to be difficult.

I could tell from Mrs. Todd's face that she knew too. We both stared at Leon who had suddenly fallen asleep or was pretending to be. Mrs. Todd carefully picked up the photographs, placing them back in the baggie. I put the one of Arthur and Daniel Slade in my purse.

Mrs. Todd placed forty dollars under the Coke bottle besides the lamp and we tiptoed out, leaving Leon Short to his memories.

39

Thrusting open the door, I marched into Lady Elsmere's farm office where June and Aspen were gathered. Both looked up in surprise.

"We're having a meeting, Josiah," cautioned June.

Ignoring her, I raised a finger at Aspen. "You lied to me."

Aspen started out of his chair, but I pushed him back down. "You lied to me and don't you dare deny it."

"I don't know what you are talking about," sputtered Aspen.

"See this cane," I said, raising my silver wolf head cane. "I am going to beat your sorry butt within an inch of your worthless hide, if you don't come clean."

"Josiah!" exclaimed June. She clawed at my arm. "What's come over you?"

"He knows who killed Arthur and has done nothing but try to throw me off the trail. Arthur's death had nothing to do with the Thin Thirty or those two men on Lakewood Drive. All that football stuff was horse manure. I'm not even sure that the sex nonsense happened. No one really saw anything concerning that. It is all conjecture and gossip.

Arthur's death had to do with money, betrayal, and revenge. It started with Arthur's dislike of one man, your partner. You've done nothing but throw me red herrings the whole time."

Lady Elsmere gasped and turned towards Aspen. "Is this true?"

Aspen said nothing, but kept his eye on my cane.

When he didn't respond, June cried out, "Go ahead. Beat him, Josiah. Beat him good."

I brought the cane down hard about Aspen's knees.

He howled out in pain. "Are you crazy, you stupid bitch!"

"Hit him again!" cried June.

I raised the cane again.

Aspen grabbed my wrist. "Okay. Okay. No more. I'll talk."

Satisfied, I pulled up a chair. June was seething with fury but trying to control herself.

"What do you want to know?"

"Neither of you two told me that the Royal Blue Stables was owned by you, Aspen, with a Daniel Slade, one of your football buddies from the Thin Thirty days."

"Daniel died so many years ago. I didn't think it was important," stated June. "It was ancient history. What's that got to do with Arthur?"

"You knew though, didn't you Aspen. Arthur so disliked Daniel Slade, he made sure he went down and that was the motive for his murder. You never brought up that Arthur turned you and Daniel Slade down for a loan and because of it . . . both of you lost the property."

Aspen looked at his hands, contemplating. "It was a long time ago. Arthur made good afterwards. Saved me from personal bankruptcy. Got me back on my feet again."

"But not Daniel Slade. His refusal to help Daniel might have caused Daniel's heart attack. You knew that Arthur was hung right where Daniel Slade died . . . the very exact spot. Yet you said nothing."

"Why?" asked June.

Aspen spoke with fury. "Because maybe Art had it coming. I didn't know for sure. I only suspected and if I was right I could see the murderer's point of view. Art could be a son-of-a-bitch when he wanted. He didn't have to be that harsh with Daniel. He had the money. I tried to reason with him, but he just didn't like the man and refused to help. Daniel went down the tube as a result. By denying us the loan, Art destroyed an entire family."

"And left an angry little boy behind," I said.

Aspen shook his head. "I will say no more."

"You felt guilty because you were saved and that you also turned your back on Daniel Slade."

"I did try," protested Aspen. "I tried to reason with Arthur but before I could get him to change his mind, Daniel was dead."

"And you secretly blame Arthur?"

"Yeah, so that is why I didn't say anything when Arthur died. He had it coming. After all these years, he still had it coming."

Lady Elsmere grabbed my hand. "Who? Who? What little boy?"

I shook her off. "Until I can prove it, I will keep the name to myself. You'll have to wait."

Lady Elsmere looked at us both with exasperation. "Well, hell fire and damnation!"

My thoughts exactly.

40

It was near dusk when I got out of the car. Taking a deep breath, I gathered my cane and hobbled into the Royal Blue Stables. The guard was watching TV. Knocking on the door, I asked him if Mr. Slade was around. He nodded and pointed to the back of the huge stable. Taking my time to negotiate hay bales, tack, and buckets, I finally found Daniel Slade Jr. feeding a horse. I was trembling.

"Mr. Slade?"

The son of Daniel Slade Sr. turned around and squinted. "Yeah?"

"Do you remember me? I'm Mrs. Reynolds. I own a part of Comanche."

"Not really." He patted the horse and closed the stall door. "What can I do for you?"

"I'm here to negotiate a business transaction."

Slade leaned against the stall wall. The horse could be heard munching contently from his oat bucket. "What business would that be?"

I held out the picture of his father and Arthur Greene. "I think this explains it."

Slade blanched when he saw the picture. Grabbing it, he tore it up. He wasn't leaning anymore but standing very straight, very tall, and very, very intimidating.

"That's okay. I have more copies."

"What's this about?"

"Secrets, Mr. Slade. Secrets that your father had and now you have."

"Don't know what you are talking about."

"Your father was going to shave points off a football game in 1962, but the point spread didn't turn out right. Still your father wanted his money as he had taken a chance, but Arthur Greene, the moneyman, wouldn't pay. That made your father very angry. Point one."

I took a deep breath. "Point two. When your father and his business partner, Aspen Lancaster, needed a loan, Arthur Greene wouldn't pony up because he didn't like your father. I also think he wouldn't give the loan because he wanted the relationship between Aspen and your father to falter. I think Arthur Greene was jealous. Well, as a result, your father and Aspen lose the Royal Blue, but Arthur is right there helping Aspen get back on his feet. He didn't extend that courtesy to your father. So your father, facing bankruptcy, dies from a heart attack."

I turned and pointed, "Right over there where Mr. Arthur was strangled with a bridle and hung from the rafters. I remember seeing a TV show where there was a murder in London where a man was hung from a bridge with rocks stuffed in his pockets. The police thought the manner of death had Masonic trappings. My guess is you saw the same show. I also bet your father was a Mason and that's his ring you are wearing. Classic revenge. Your father hated Arthur Greene and he passed that hate on to his children."

Slade grinned and stepped towards me. "My father never threw a game. You made that up. His remorse was more of a carnal nature so he could get enough to eat. He was starving eating that college garbage and working himself to death on that football team. Arthur owned him money for showing up at the Lakewood house and would never pay up. Arthur Greene was nothing more than a pimp and everyone thought he was such a great guy. He let my father sink for no better reason than to be an ass. Now you know. The sins of the father."

"Yes, the sins of the father visit the children seven generations." I stepped back.

"You can't prove a thing, lady. What do you want? Money? I haven't got two pennies. My bank account is overdrawn now."

"The boy remembers. He will identify you."

"No one is going to pay attention to the ramblings of a boy."

"You must have threatened Arthur about telling about his involvement with recruiting young men if he didn't give you money. But Arthur turned the tables on you.

"He was too rich, too powerful to really give a damn about something that happened over 40 years ago. He could treat it as a joke, a college prank and wait to ride out the scandal, but it would humiliate your family. So it was Arthur threatening you that he would tell about your father and you begging him not to.

"Then you saw Linc. He ran away and fell. Arthur had his back to the boy, but upon hearing him fall, went to help him. As he was leaning over Linc, his fountain pen fell out of his pocket . . . this fountain pen." I held up the dirty gold pen.

"Seeing an opportunity, you hit Arthur on the head, strangled him, and then hung him . . . right where your father had had his heart attack."

"Everyone who was involved is dead."

"Not Aspen. He loved Arthur and when he finds out for sure that you killed his childhood friend, he'll turn his back on you. He will tell people the entire story because he knows how everyone was involved in the past. What would be worse – being fodder for some oversexed men or possibly having shaved points during a game?"

Dan Slade's face was a mask of fury. He started towards me.

"Oh no," was all I could muster as I started moving back. I fell over something and cried out. Looking up, I saw Dan Slade was about to pummel my face with a shovel, which he held over his head.

"God no!" I screamed before I heard . . .

"Hold it right there, boy. Don't want to put holes in you just to save Josiah Reynolds."

Out of the corner of my eyes, I beheld Detective Goetz pointing a gun at Slade while two police officers advanced. One held out handcuffs.

Slade threw the shovel down and let out a horrible cry as he was led away.

Goetz tried to help me up but I cried out too.

"What is it?"

"I think I broke my leg. I can't get up."

Goetz called for an ambulance.

"Did we get him?"

"Don't think so. He didn't really confess."

"Isn't trying to bash my head in a sort of confession?"

"Nope. Maybe you just irritated him that much."

"I broke my leg for nothing?"

"Well, I couldn't very well let him bash your head in."

"You'd have been doing me a favor."

"Shut up."

"What?"

"Shut up. I hate stupid talk like that."

I did shut up.

Not because I wanted to, but because I had passed out.

41

Goetz had just left the hospital.

He had come to inform me that Slade had finally confessed to the murder of Arthur Aaron Greene III. Slade could not explain why Arthur Greene had disliked his father so, but that his refusal to help had cost the Slade family much. The court had ordered an psychological evaluation for Slade.

Goetz was barely out the door before Shaneika started in on me.

Handing me a tissue box before she continued. "Are you going to stop crying, so I can finish?"

"How much more is there?" I asked pressing a button for the nurse.

"We gotta get a defense here," complained Shaneika. She looked imploringly at Matt.

Matt held my hand. "Look, Rennie, you've got to be strong."

"You haven't called me Rennie in the longest time." Matt called me Rennie after the actor Michael Rennie, who played in *The Day The Earth Stood Still.* I helped him win a bet on what Michael Rennie's commands were to the robot. It was how we met.

"Woman, you've got to focus," Matt implored.

"Matt, this is useless. She's floating in the sky with pain killers."

"Yes, Josiah must be very happy that she's got all the pain medication she wants."

"I understand exactly what you both are saying. Ellen smells blood with O'nan making a fuss and thinks she can squeeze another dime out of me. I hate her. I wish she were dead."

Shaneika closed the door to my hospital room. "Don't say things like that. You know better."

"The Butterfly is in my name. My name is on that deed and only my name. I designed the Butterfly – not Brannon. He only built it for me. The Butterfly is mine. How can she lay claim to it?"

"Try to understand. The case she is making is that the Butterfly is not just another house, but an institution – an icon. Because everyone thinks that Brannon designed it, his only son should have a portion or say into what happens to the house. You will die, eventually, but the house will go on. It will probably be a foundation or a trust that sees to it."

"My will gives it to Asa. It will be Asa's to do with it what she wants."

Matt intervened, "But Ellen is making the case that a portion of the house belongs to her son as it is an important historical piece of architecture, the first of its kind."

I started to cry. "That woman is going to be the death of me."

"I'm sorry but it looks as though there is a mounted effort to hem you in, Josiah. Ellen must have been working on this for a long time with her friends," said Matt.

"And now that O'nan is free on bail, she thinks she can rattle your cage."

"And she is doing a fine job of it," I whined. "What do I do? The wolves are at the door. If O'nan doesn't cut my throat while I'm in the hospital, I've got to deal with Ellen when I get out."

Matt looked at Shaneika. "We are working on a counter defense, but you have to stay cool, man. Don't make things worse. Stay away from her and make no statements to your friends about Ellen. Mum's the word."

I nodded in agreement. The door opened and a nurse brought in a tray of food. Baby swill is what I call it. Jell-O and something that looked like brown tapioca pudding. Yuck.

Matt glanced at the tray and reared back. "Is that all they're feeding you?"

"They are practically starving me to death."

Shaneika responded, "Well, I am going home to my Mama's cooking." She grinned, "Good luck eating that."

With that, she left with Matt following close behind. He turned, giving me a cheeky grin. I could tell Matt was going to hit Shaneika up for a dinner invitation.

I was starving. I gulped down the pudding, but couldn't bring myself to eat the Jell-O. Pushing the tray away, I settled in for a quick snooze.

Hearing the door open, I struggled to sit up. "Now what?"

"Hello, Babe."

I couldn't believe my eyes.

Standing in front of my bed was . . . Jake.

42

Shaneika, Mrs. Todd, Jake, and I sat in our box seats at Keeneland for the Breeders' Futurity Stakes.   I had to keep pushing the feathers from Mrs. Todd's hat away from my face until I plucked them out and threw them on the floor when she wasn't looking.

Shaneika looked strained but Mike Connor gave a big smile and clasped her hand.

Mrs. Todd gave me a quick look as if to say, "What is this?"

I just shrugged my shoulders.

The horses started to make their entrance onto the track. I bit my lip as Comanche was led on to the turf.

The jockey had trouble getting him into the starter gate. Suddenly the bell went off and the gates opened. Horses like colorful birds flew out of the metal cages and raced down the dirt track. Hooves clamoring on the dirt track sounded like heartbeats. The crowd roared in anticipation.

Everyone jumped to their feet. Matt handed me his binoculars while Franklin screamed in my ear. I barely took a breath as I watched as the horses turn the corner and were heading home. Jake set calmly in his seat.

"Come on, Comanche," I yelled. "Move your bloomin' arse. Run!"

"Make your move!" screamed Franklin, jumping up and down, hanging on to Matt's arm. "Make your move."

Mrs. Todd was hopping in her brand new black pumps, grabbing her now featherless hat.

I looked over and saw that Shaneika had her eyes closed.

That was good as Comanche came in . . . dead last.

EPILOGUE

The dark clad figure pulled out the wires to the security box. Deftly, the intruder cut the correct wire to silence the alarm. Then going around to the southwest part of the huge mansion built in 1832; the thief skillfully unlocked the side porch door and stepped into the library.

Hearing a dog growling in the hallway, the thief threw a piece of meat towards the hall and stood patiently until the dog ate the meat and a moment later groggily stumbled, falling asleep. It would sleep for several hours from the drug administered to the meat but would wake up unharmed.

The thief looked for a wall safe behind paintings and even tapped on the walnut paneling. Finding nothing, the dark figure concentrated on the desk, taking pictures of any checks, bank statements, investments that could be found. Then she copied the computer files onto a flash drive.

Several drawers were locked but took the thief only seconds to break them open. Finding a handgun, the thief put it into a black bag; also several silver trophies from a bookshelf.

Silently investigating the house, the thief stole an antique silver tea set in the dining room and turned towards the front parlor. There the thief moved to the Duveneck painting hanging over the mantel. With quiet efficiency, the thief broke the frame and then cut the painting from its stretcher. Rolled, the painting was placed in a tube the thief had brought.

Both the painting and the bag with the silver were lowered out a window.

Now unencumbered, the thief studied the massive staircase. Making a calculated decision, the thief leaped up the stairs, taking three steps at a time. Hiding in the shadows of the hallway, the thief saw that most of the upstairs doors were open.

Seeing what looked like a nightlight dimly peeping into the hallway, the thief surmised that it came from a child's room and headed for it.

The thief was right.

A boy, wearing Spider Man pajamas, lay asleep in a bed designed to look like a racecar. The thief studied the child's features. Suddenly the thief's hand shot out, but only to pull the blanket over the little boy.

The black, sleek figure pulled itself away and went to look for the mother's room. Going next door, the thief discovered the mother of the boy asleep in her king size bed. She was wearing shorts and a sports bra. Like the boy, she had thrown off her blanket and lay sprawled across the bed, lightly snoring. A purse hung off a chair.

The thief claimed it and then went directly to a jewelry box sitting on the vanity and took it downstairs. Pouring the contents of both the purse and the box onto the couch, the thief picked up several pieces of jewelry and a wallet, only to flee out the side door. The thief was careful to lock it again.

Picking up the bag and tube, the thief absconded into the woods and to a country road where a car was waiting. Flinging the goods in the trunk, the thief turned off the night goggles, throwing them on top of the sack. Starting with gloves, the thief took off dark clothing, revealing a casual fall outfit. The dark clothing was stuffed into a garbage bag and securely tied. The thief let long dark hair escape from a confining cap and got in the car, quietly shutting the door.

The driver looked at his boss. "Twenty-five minutes. What took you so long?"

"The painting was more trouble than I anticipated," lied Asa. "Let's move on down the road."

The car sped down Old Frankfort Pike with its lights off until it cut over the road to Midway.

Asa leaned back in the seat, smiling to herself. Ellen was going to be distracted as she was going to spend a great deal of time cleaning up identity theft which was going to start occurring tonight. As for the jewelry and silver, Asa would stash it in her New York apartment's safe until she could have something made from the stolen loot. The credit cards would be given to her driver.

Forty-five minutes later, Asa boarded a Piper from a private airstrip in Scott County and flew to New York.

The employee made several outlandish purchases from Ellen's iPhone with her credit cards and then dropped the cards on the floor of a drinking establishment in Covington.

Josiah Reynolds slept fitfully in her bed, never knowing that her daughter had been in Kentucky.

BONUS

AN EXCITING CHAPTER FROM

"DEATH BY BOURBON"

PROLOGUE

Doreen Doris Mayfield DeWitt tapped her tapered glossy nails on the gleaming end table while watching the woman pace before her. Although she felt like swiping the woman with her claws, she remained passive, watching as her guest spewed forth countless words trying to explain her situation.

"You see, Doreen, I simply can't go on like this. I mean . . .well, I didn't mean to fall in love with Addison. It just happened. So I'm going to have to renege on our little agreement. It simply wouldn't be right."

"You mean the agreement where I paid you to seduce Addison and provide evidence of adultery so I wouldn't have to give him part of my fortune according to my prenup with him."

Lacey Bridges batted her large blue eyes. "Well, I never asked you why you wanted me to seduce Addison. Is that why? You want to divorce Addison. Well, that's wonderful because I want to marry Addison. See – it works out for everyone."

"Except for evidence of adultery or abuse, I would have to pay Addison a substantial sum of my own money – my family's money."

"You could always say that he hit you."

"Don't be ridiculous," snapped Doreen. "No one would believe that."

"Well, I don't know what to say. This is a pickle for you."

"Let's start with the money I've already paid you and the video you were supposed to make for me."

Lacey laughed. "Well, the money is gone . . . for clothes you know. And the tapes – well, I had to destroy those, you see."

Doreen sighed. "Do you always have to start a sentence with well?"

"What?"

"Never mind."

Lacey simpered. "It wouldn't do well to insult me, Doreen. I haven't told Addison the truth yet, but I will if you keep on pushing me."

"Afraid that he might recoil from such a gold digger as you?"

"He would forgive me eventually but it would slow up the divorce, that's for sure." Lacey searched in her purse for lipstick. "Well, the way I look at it, we can all get what we want. You get rid of Addison and I get him with a little bit of money. Oh, come off it. I'm sure you can spare some cash on Addison. Surely you want him to go out in style?" Lacey opened her compact and smeared on dark red lipstick. Dropping the compact and lipstick back into her purse, she stood satisfied at both her appearance and negotiation. "I am sure we can work this out to both our mutual satisfactions. All of this depends of just how badly you want to divorce Addison, doesn't it."

Lacey placed a card on Doreen's antique end table. "Here's where you can reach me. I'm sure you'll see that I am right after thinking about it. Don't rise, please. I'll see myself out." She air kissed Doreen and then pranced out of the room.

Upon hearing the front door slam shut, Doreen stared into the fireplace losing herself to the dancing flames thinking, thinking, thinking.

She'd be damned before she gave one red cent to that worthless English hustler she married. Absently-mindedly she fingered the heavy gold ring on her right hand until she finally felt its weight pull on her. Lifting her hand up to her face, she opened the ring's secret compartment and smiled. Good thing she had always liked history or she never would had purchased a ring supposedly owned by Lucrezia Borgia.

Doreen laughed. "Now what would Lucrezia do in my circumstance?"

It was very late when Doreen finally went to bed but not before she had concocted a plan. She would get rid of Addison and his obnoxious little bitch too. And no one would know that it was she that pulled the strings of a little murder about to take place in the calm green rolling hills of the Bluegrass.

Kentucky is not called the dark and bloody ground for nothing.